two times eleven

gong'an
öffentliche aushänge

jürgen rahn

Aus einem interview des "Marburger Tageblatt"
der Wochenendausgabe 16.10.2021

MT: *Ihr neustes Werk ist mir rätselhafter denn je, schreiben viel, holen sich noch selber ein.*
JR: richtig, habe mir Hui-Shis These, "ich gehe heute nach Yue, bin aber gestern bereits dort angekommen", zu eigen gemacht.
MT: *Sie sagten, dies sei die Dokumentatiom einer Sammlung von ihnen anonym verschickter Postkarten.*
JR: Insgesamt 22 DIN-lang Karten an circa neunzig Adressaten.
Ist in "two times eleven" eine Zahlenmystik verborgen?
"Two times eleven, makes twenty two", ein variabler Bluesvers aus "Ain't nobody's biz-ness", Die Post hatte 2019 das Porto für Postkarten um "three times eleven" Prozent erhöht. Das war der Garaus angesichts sowieso schon grenzwertiger Kosten.
Wie sind die Abbildungen auf der Adressseite der Karten zu verstehen? Mich verunsichern sie über gebühr, überhaupt etwas zu verstehen.
Gar nicht, sind damit auf gutem Weg zu erkennen, der nützliche Sinn bringt die Welt nicht in gewünschte Ordnung. Letztlich diente das immer nur dem Nutzen der Herrschenden, bliebe immer alles Zwecklose und Widersinnige ausgeschlossen . Erhalten wir diese Quelle der Inspiration und Freiheit.
Seltsame Freiheit, wozu dient sie?
Öffnet Horizonte, von unseren Scheuklappen verdeckt. Im chinesischen "Chan" wurden schon vor Ende des ersten Jahrtausends in den Klöstern solche Aushänge *"gong'an"* als befreiende Kopfnüsse gesammelt, Beispiele, einige Gewissheiten orthodoxer buddhistischer Lehre, deren Auslegung der Sutren, zu unterwandern.
Das entzieht sich meiner Kenntnis, aber eine Kellerassel als Pilger, ein Feuerkäfer als Klostervorsteher, eine sich von Tinte und Druckerschwärze ernährende Orchidee, unverständliche Dispute gelehrter Insekten, all das wird wohl kaum in der von ihnen genannten Tradition stehen.
In der Tradition der Fabel. Reminiszenzen finden sich schon im daoistischen Chuang-tzu,
Was ich nicht alles erst einmal "googeln" müsste.
Bitte nicht. Lesen sie lieber für zwei Minuten laut die Namen einer beliebigen Seite eines beliebigen Telefonbuchs, ihnen geht's gleich wieder besser.
Ich weiß, "googeln" bequemt die Flüchtigkeit der Meinungen.
Sie sagen es, Die *"gong'an"* sind Lehrbeispiele der anderen Art, Das H durch E ersetzt, die LEERE ist doch eine gute Grundlage. Angesichts unserer Sterblichkeit ist das eine nicht erst sich zuletzt stellende Frage, was das Ganze denn nun alles zu bedeuten hatte.

In früheren Gesprächen habe ich sie selten gerne ausreden lassen. War froh sagen zu können, "der Speicher ist voll", Das ist zwar jetzt tatsächlich, muss sagen, leider der Fall, was ich diesmal bedaure, und sie wissen schon, das übliche Honorar, eine Flasche Whiskey.

two times eleven

gong'an
öffentliche aushänge

Bibliografische Information der Deutschen Nationalbibliothek: Die Deutsche Nationalbibliothek verzeichnet diese Publikation in der Deutschen Nationalbibliografie; detaillierte bibliografische Daten sind im Internet über dnb.dnb.de abrufbar.

»two times eleven«
gong'an – öffentliche aushänge

Zweitveröffentlichung 2023
die originalen Postkartentexte wurden überarbeitet
ISBN 9783739242644

Korrektorat Hans Peter Thurn

Herstellung und Verlag: BoD – Books on Demand, Norderstedt

Texte und Abbildungen
Copyright © 2021 jürgen rahn

Weitere Veröffentlichungen bei BoD

»versgedanken – angesichts des marsgottes neusprech« 2022
ISBN 9783756842322

»riding stellar winds« 2021
ISBN 9783754320846

»versgedanken – unplugged & offline« 2021
ISBN 9783755756682

form, or matter, is empitiness
emptiness is not different from form
nor is form differet from emptiness
indeed, emptiness is form

(aus dem "Sutra of Transcendental Wisdom")

… Then I'd run these words
through my mind to train myself:
"I am emptiness
I am not different from emptiness
neither is emptiness different from me
indeed emptiness is me."

… I wasn't exactly unconscious of the fact
that I had a good warm fire to return after
these midnight meditations

(Jack Kerouac in "The Dharma Bums" Kapitel 20)

öffentlicher aushang 101
hohes gras und weiße alpengipfel
bearbeitet und *kommentiert*
vom brunnenfrosch »Kleiner Tellerrand«

das beispiel

Krätze, eine pilgernde kellerassel, stattet dem orangefarbenen feuerkäfer Johann Custos, in dessen entlegener stille klause in der krone eines korallenbaums, einen ersten besuch ab.
"Woher kommst du des weges?" fragt der eremit.
"Über stock und stein, bergeshöhe und meeresufer."
Nun ja der pilger fürchtet die fallstricke, steckt er damit nicht schon im tiefen gras?
Johann Custos, "wie findet sich da der richtige weg?"
Der hausherr irrt nun unversehens selbst durchs grasgestrüpp.
Der pilger, "querfeldein."
Statt zu schweigen überzieht Krätze den schnee nun noch mit reif.
Der klausner, "hohes gras und weiße alpengipfel."
Der pilger schweigt, zu spät, reif auf schnee und was dann?

gesang der grille Tritonus

der augen wimpernschlag
züngeln der meereswellen am strand
reif überzieht den schnee
endloser sturz ins gras
dort
und nirgendwo

»doch mein sein Ist fest umrissen«
tönt laut ein stein
am fuß des gebirgsfelsens
»erbarmen«
stöhnt der weiße gipfel
gestört in seiner wolkenruhe
sein stirnrunzeln
löst eine schneelawine aus

beständig ist nur der weg, der atem des windes, der rollende donner, weder fels noch schnee, noch korallenbaum, noch gras.

öffentlicher aushang 102
begegnung eines gedankens' und einer feder

bearbeitet und *kommentiert*
vom brunnenfrosch »Kleiner Tellerrand«

das beispiel

Johann Custos, der feuerkäfer gewährt Krätze, der kellerassel, ein weiteres gespräch.
Der eremit hat eine frage: "Ein gedanke begegnet einer feder. Gibt es dazu etwas zu sagen?"
Krätze zögert nicht, "die feder hält ihn fest."
Meint der wirklich nur die feder oder denkt er mehr an sich selbst, das unsagbare zu wahren? Da hat der sich aber viel vorgenommen!
Der eremit erwidert, "in dem morgendlichen gefunkel der tauperlen auf den gräsern siehst du den polarstern nicht."
Welche lehre soll denn das dem jungen gast werden, warum ihn nicht auf der stelle vom baum hinunter ins tiefe gras stoßen.
Krätze gibt nicht auf, "was aber sieht der meister?"
Der antwortet, "ein federleichtes wölkchen, das sich im blau des himmels auflöst."
Hat der eremit sich nun nicht wie ein widder mit seinen hörnern in einer hecke verfangen, oder will er sich auf diese weise der anfangsfrage entledigen, versöhnlich wieder zurück in das hier und jetzt?

gesang der grille Tritonus

will sich nichts entgehen lassen
Alles fassen im einzigen SINN
der vogel kommt durch fliegen ins unheil
da läßt sich nichts machen
eingefangen mit einer einzigen frage
umgarnt von der namen gaukelei
spiegelfechtereien
sie verfliegen
federleichte wölkchen im blau des himmels
gut gesagt?

Wer glaubt denn auch, im traum wäre eine brille dienlich? Gibt es doch nur einen weg, frei von allem SINN. Jeder poet kann ein lied davon singen.

öffentlicher aushang 103
Osramus' gipfel der erhabenheit

bearbeitet und *kommentiert*
vom brunnenfrosch »Kleiner Tellerrand«

das beispiel

Die pilgernde kellerassel Krätze und ihr treuer begleiter Osramus, der leuchtkäfer, sie warten beide darauf, nach einbruch der nacht weiter zu ziehen, auf diesem, von Wu-wei der eintagsfliege, angeratenen weg richtung westen.

Tasteten sich eben noch verirrte, zittrige sonnenlichtfinger durch das tiefe gras, so wölbt sich nun, von osten mächtig aufsteigend, der funkelnde nachthimmel unaufhaltsam in die höhe, und mit dem licht weichen auch die letzten schatten.

Osramus: "Diese stunde, ist das nicht der gipfel des erhabenen?"
Krätze: "Dem gemüt blühen trügerische blumen. Pass' nur auf, dass du beim runterfallen weich landest."

Ob die unserem blick nur langsam ihrer wege ziehenden sterne, oder das von den herbstwinden flüchtig über mein brunnenloch hinweg- oder gar hineingewirbelte laub, nichts da, an erhabenheit in der natur. Kein groß oder klein. Kein bestirnter Himmel über mir, noch ein moralisches Gesetz in mir. Niemals halten ferne sehnsuchtsorte den erwartungen stand. Nach manchen weiten reisen mit der wolke Adagio, wieder zurück in meinem brunnen, versäumt hatte ich doch letztlich nichts.

auf einladung der grille Tritonus:

gesang des Heinrich Heine

Ich verbrachte fast die Hälfte
Jener Nacht auf dem Balkone.
Neben mir stand Juliette
Und betrachtete die Sterne.

Seufzend sprach sie: "Ach, die Sterne
Sind am schönsten in Paris,
Wenn sie dort, des Winterabends,
In dem Straßenkot sich spiegeln.

(Atta Troll - Caput II)

öffentlicher aushang 104
wolken in bedrängnis

bearbeitet
vom brunnenfrosch »Kleiner Tellerrand«

das beispiel

Dunkle wolken haben den hohen himmel überzogen und hängen nun tief zwischen den bergen, als wäre ihnen aller mut zur weiterreise genommen. Der meereshorizont, der sich von seinen pflichten losgesagt hat, und nun die beiden pilger, Krätze, die kellerassel, und den sie begleitenden leuchtkäfer Osramus, auf seinen schultern trägt, um den beiden ein stück des weges voran zu helfen, steigt mit ihnen umsichtig durch steil aufragende klüfte eines himmelhohen gebirges.

Krätze behagt die reise durchs gebirge nicht so recht. Die enge seines vergangenen kellerdaseins hat ihm zu lange eine behagliche sicherheit vorgegaukelt. Es inzwischen besser zu wissen reicht da nicht, und so fragt sie misstrauisch:
"Seltsame geräusche um uns, was bedeuten sie?"
"Der nachhall fernen donners", sagt Osramus.
"Wie das denn, ohne blitz?" soviel meint Krätze nun doch zu wissen.
"In einem anderen tal", erklärt ihr begleiter, "den wolken hier geht's auch nicht viel besser, sie sind ganz schön in der klemme, und fallwinde pfeifen im fels."
Der meereshorizont mischt sich ein: "Ihr hört vieles und begreift einiges, aber durchdringt ihr dieses auch?"
"Ist was dahinter?" will Krätze wissen.
Der meereshorizont: "Das geräusch ungefasster weite und unbegrezter stille."

gesang der grille Tritonus

ein aufgerichteter horizont in der landschaft
eine strichfigur
über die höhen des gebirges
christophorus - überwärts und niederwärts
hinter flüchtigen ängsten
der dauer stille
keine ursache und wirkung
des Parmenides kosmos

öffentlicher aushang105
Wu-wei's wurzellose worte

bearbeitet und *kommentiert*
vom brunnenfrosch »Kleiner Tellerrand«

das beispiel

Bevor sie ihre reise nach westen antrat, traf die kellerassel Krätze ihren mentor Wu-wei, die eintagsfliege.
"Wie erklärst du dir das?" fragt Wu-wei, "übermorgen wirst du dich, von mir ermutigt, auf diesen weg begeben. Wie ich sehe, du hast heute schon einen großteil des weges zurückgelegt."
"Das soll wohl eher sagen, ich hab schon den ersten schritt vorgelegt?"
"Wenn du gestern ankommen willst, dann heißt es jetzt eher, es gilt noch einiges nachzulegen."

Worte ihrer schale entkernen, diese eintagsfliege versteht sich wohl bestens darauf, zerschlägt das möbilar im denkstübchen.

Daraufhin ist Wu-wei verschwunden, wie von der zeit verschluckt, oder war's nur ein traum? Krätze´s begleiter, der leuchtkäfer Osramus hat das genau verfolgt, "wir können wohl schlecht das gleiche träumen."
Krätze kratzte sich am kopf. Der leuchtkäfer: "Wenn Wu-wei versteht, die zeit zu verknoten, könnte er uns doch helfen, zum rechten augenblick vorgezogener zeit am ende des regenbogens zu sein, ehe dieser sich über den himmel spannt, ihm den versteckten glückstopf rechtzeitig zu entreißen? Das wäre ein lohnendes ziel unserer reise."

Die beiden pilger wandern unverzagt im tiefen gras, träume überwärts sind da leicht gefasst.

gesang der grille Tritonus

ohne pfeil, der bogenschuss
worten, die wurzeln durchtrennen
haargenau spaltet Wu-wei die zeit
aus vielerlei, einerlei und keinerlei
aus dem heute erhebt sich ein déjà vu
aus dem morgen entspringt das gestern
we´ve forgotten things
we´ve never known

Ein uns bekannter eintrag von lieutenant Ripley im logbuch der rettungskapsel der kurz zuvor atomisierten Nostromo: "I should reach the frontier in about six weeks, with a little luck, the network will pick me up." Siebenundfünfzig jahre später wurde sie gefunden. Nicht gealtert, ihre tochter, eine weißhaarige greisin.

öffentlicher aushang 106
wer hält sie denn gefangen?
bearbeitet und *kommentiert*
vom brunnenfrosch »Kleiner Tellerrand«
das beispiel

In jenen abgelegenen, verlassenen kreuzgang des *vacanti*, der innenhof von allerlei wildwuchs längst in besitzt genommen, alles mauerwerk ebenfalls überwuchert, verirrt sich niemand mehr, es sei denn ihn bewegt die seltene absicht, Johann Custos, den feuerkäfer, hoch oben im geäst seines korallenbaums zu besuchen.

"Was ist da grad' von draußen zu hören?" fragt dieser seinen besucher Krätze, die pilgernde kellerassel.

Warum fragt er das überhaupt, weiß er doch sehr wohl, es ist nur der an- und abebbende wellengang mönchischer gesänge, der gelegentlich herüberschwappt, aber von der hiesigen stille sogleich geschluckt.

Krätze blickt derweil versonnen den über ihnen im blau des himmels dahinziehenden weißen wölkchen nach, "Sie sind so federleicht, und doch höre ich ein lamentieren, als trügen sie ein große last."
"Sie bitten um erlösung!"
"Wer kann sie denn gefangen halten?"
"Ihr glauben oder unglauben, einerlei."
"Aber sie segeln so frei durch das blau des himmels ..."
… was immer Krätze noch sagen will, ihr gegenüber holt zu einem das gespräch rabiat verkürzenden stoß aus, sie in die tiefe zu befördern; wenn nicht der pilger sich zusammengerollt hätte, statt dessen nun dem meister nachblickt, der, das gleichgewicht verloren, nun selbst unten im grasgestrüpp landet.

Beide klatschen mit einer hand ins blaue.

gesang der grille Tritonus

rudern im takt des trommelschlags
auf der galeere weiß jeder um sein los
einer ersten frage kleine differenz
am ende weit auseinander gedriftet
durchs tiefe gras irren
sehen einander im nahen nicht mehr
wer befreit wen und wovon
zurück ins hier und jetzt tut not

öffentlicher aushang 107
Piedplat und der stoff der träume

bearbeitet und *kommentiert*
vom brunnenfrosch »Kleiner Tellerrand«

das beispiel

Die dickkopffliege Piedplat, ein streifenpolizist, hat der, in seinem revier, dem Bois de Brume, ihr zugelaufenen seltsamen orichdeenpflanze in einem mit guter gartenerde gefüllten tontopf verdünnte tinte zu trinken gegeben, um ihr den appetit auf druckerschwärze zu nehmen.

"Stell mir doch einfach das offene tintenfass auf den tisch, oder lass mich zeitung lesen", monierte die fremde.

Diese rede müssen wir uns wohl eher als stumme gedankenübertragung vorstellen.

"Ich möchte nicht dass du herumtaperst, in meinen romanen blätterst, nicht bevor ich sie selbst gelesen habe. Du lässt mir ja nichts übrig."
"Aber sie sind so nahrhaft und von besonderem geschmack."
"So wie ich am tisch esse, so nimmst du bitte deine mahlzeiten in deinem topf ein, und gedrucktes naschen gibt es nicht."
"Was immer dir das gedruckte bedeutet, mich nährt es."
"Du hinterlässt nur leere papierseiten. Deine tintenration ist mehr als großzügig. Pflanzenart ist diese art ernährung schon mal gar nicht. Und überhaupt, für pflanzen gehört es sich, sesshaft zu sein."
"Ich bin nicht du, und du weißt nicht, wie es ist, ich zu sein."

Behaupten, alles sei subjektiv, wie paradox, kann das denn zugleich objektive gültigkeit beanspruchen?

Piedplat: "Du hast zu häufig in der bibliothek des Vacanti heimlich in den bücherregalen herumgestöbert. Wenn du dir dabei nicht ganz schön den magen verdorben hast."

gesang der grille Tritonus

How does a table know how it is
to be a dog running free ?
When plants drag out their roots
walking´ round in a spooky manner,
when narrative becomes plain fiction
but thoughts still cast a light on reality
at it´s best - we´ll accept it:
"the willing suspension of disbelief" *

*James Taylor Coleridge

öffentlicher aushang 108
was gibt es neues?
bearbeitet und *kommentiert*
vom brunnenfrosch »Kleiner Tellerrand«

das beispiel

Die kleine wolke Adagio hat sich vor dem ungehaltenen nordwind in die luftigen höhen der schon ewig verlassenen wolkenkuckucksburg geflüchtet und besucht dort den einsam hausenden freund, einen starenvogel. Yussef J. Beo. Beide freuen sich über dieses wiedersehen.

"Oh, mein lieber Adagio, was gibt es neues von dort unten?"
"Als künstler weißt du doch, wie flüchtig schatten sind."
"Ausgerechnet eine wolke sagt das? Neeh, ne ne, jaa, ja ja."
"Wolken sind uhren, hat ein kluger mann mal gesagt."
"Nee,nee neeh, wie kann ich dann überhaupt sicher sein dass du wirklich der unwägbare Adagio bist und nicht ein mechanismus?"
"Denk an meinen letzten besuch mit dem Brunnenfrosch. Keine andere wolke wüsste davon zu sprechen."
"Jaaa ja jaa … neeeh, ne ne … ja … "
"Also, dann war´s das wieder für heute?"
"Neeeh ne neee, jaahh ja ja … ne, nehhhhh …"

Das mantra für den direkten draht zum schöpfer, dharma oder dao, auch gibt es die rede von, "euer ja sei ein ja und euer nein sei ein nein". Sofort nach Yussef J. Beos begrüßung hat Adagio sich in ihren erörterungen hoffnungslos verheddert.

gesang der grille Tritonus

einst der vögel trutzburg
stadt und staat zwischen himmel und erde
der götter und gedanken flüge zu besteuern
die vögel wollten zu hoch hinaus
nun eine verlassene oase der stille
schattenlos und zeitlos
sagt mir
was interessieren neuigkeiten dort?
neuschnee auf raureif und wer
packt noch was drauf?
jaah jaaa jah, neeh neh neeeeee

öffentlicher aushang 109
der leere eine heimat
bearbeitet und *kommentiert*
vom brunnenfrosch »Kleiner Tellerrand«

das beispiel

Bel Nimra, ein scharlachroter feuerkäfer, hausherr des Vacanti, begrüßt in der eingangshalle des instituts einen geladenen künstler.
Vor einer überdimensionierten voluminösen, hohen und mit malereien der landschaft versehenen porzellanvase, mittig zwischen einem beidseitigen treppenaufgang postiert, bleiben hausherr und gast für einen moment stehen.
Bel Nimra: "Gib´ es nur zu, dem künstler gefällt die vase nicht."
Künstler: "Von immensem ausmaß, abgesehen von ihrem ursprünglichen zweck, aber auch gewaltig hohl, ich ..."
"Vermagst du es denn, der leere dieser vase eine bessere heimat zu geben?"
Künstler: "Wenn sie sich sicher in meine werkstatt transportieren ließe, dann wollte ich mein bestes tun."
Der hausherr zögert nicht, eine order an eine der wachen, und kurz darauf wird die vase vor beider augen in stücke zerschlagen.
Der künstler, irritiert: "Und wie soll ich nun an der leere maß nehmen?"
"Aber nur zu, sie ist noch hier, lass dich nicht foppen, ich lass dir zeit. Fenster und türen bleiben geschlossen, sie kann dir nicht entwischen."

Bel Nimra hat seinen gast auf brüchig dünnes eis geführt. Die lehre der leere, da endet jede kunst.

gesang der eintagsfliege Wu-wei

die vase war das maß der leere
so bleiben es auch ihre scherben

gestalt ist leere
leere unterscheidet sich nicht von gestalt
noch dass sich gestalt von leere unterscheidet
in der tat
leere ist gestalt

öffentlicher aushang 110
mit nichts zu besuch

bearbeitet und *kommentiert*
vom brunnenfrosch »Kleiner Tellerrand«

hinweis

Ein geladener gast erscheint mit nichts. Ob zu üppig, oder eher dürftig, das fragt sich jetzt.

das beispiel

"Bester freund, mein dank für die einladung, stehe nun aber verlegen vor ihnen, komme ich doch mit nichts."
"Macht nichts, werfen sie es weg, ihre anwesenheit bleibt mir eine ehre."
"Wegwerfen, wie denn? Nehmen sie es nicht an, mir bliebe nur, mit nichts wieder umzukehren."
"Und wenn ich das nichts also annähme?"
"Wie denn überreichen ? Es ist doch kein blumenstrauß."
"Stecken wir´s dennoch zu den blumen dort drüben in die vase, für nichts dürfte sich wohl noch reichlich platz finden."
"Sehr unangemessen, das universum passt doch auch nicht in ein blumenstillleben."

Dem nichts wird immer unbehaglicher zu mute. Kurzerhand, mir nichts dir nichts, schaltet es diesen dialog in einer zeitschleife kurz, weshalb auch nicht überliefert ist, wann und ob überhaupt diese begegnung je stattgefunden hat.

"Bester freund, mein dank für die einladung, stehe nun aber verlegen vor ihnen, komme ich doch mit nichts."
"Macht nichts, werfen sie es weg, ihre anwesenheit bleibt mir eine ehre."

Ach ja, wo war ich gleich, frage ich mich also, wie kommt das nichts überhaupt zu etwas, und der astronom des Vacanti behauptet sogar, das universum passe in eine nussschale.

gesang der grille Tritonus

alle greifen beim nichts daneben
erst der diabolus (in musica)
dem gesang entsprungen
hat die anfängliche symmetrie durchbrochen
die musik beflügelt
die welt zu erschaffen

öffentlicher aushang 111
höhe ohne ausblick

bearbeitet und *kommentiert*
vom brunnenfrosch »Kleiner Tellerrand«

hinweis

Vorauseilende erwartungen und kurzatmige zeit. Anfangs nur ein leichter webfehler, am ende trägt dieser teppich nicht weit.

das beispiel

"Nun bin ich voller erwartungen, den beschwerlichen weg bis hier herauf gestiegen, steile pfade des hochwaldes, schmale stege zwischen engem fels, über stürzende wasser und bin doch nur in ein weiteres tal ohne blick in die ferne gelangt", so stöhnt der wanderer, nachdem ihn ein kuhhirte vor seiner hütte freundlich willkommen geheißen hat.

"Die erwartungen waren wohl zu schweres gepäck", bemerkt dieser fürsorglich, "legen sie erst einmal ab und ruhen sich aus. Sie sind diese höhe nicht gewohnt."
"Und was hilft mir die höhe ohne ausblick ?"
"So sind sie alle, die vorbeikommen und die stille nicht hören können, aber von der ferne träumen."
"Sie haben seltsam reden. Nur ist die sonne schon längst über ihren zenit hinaus gewandert, und für die rückkehr läuft mir die zeit davon."
"Sie wird sich von selbst wieder einfinden. Nehmen sie dann getrost ihre zeit fest bei der hand, und kehren sie zusammen um, ehe die dröhnende stille sie beide verschluckt."

Eine in der nähe weidende kuh muuuhhhht. Gravitätisch verneigen sich die gipfel der umliegenden berge.

Nicht die stille, sondern die illusion einer welt en miniature suchen, wie soll das die last des lebens dort unten mindern können ?

gesang der grille Tritonus

also sage ich
ferne gibt es nur in der leere der stille
die leere der stille unterscheidet sich nicht von ferne
noch dass sich ferne von der leere der stille unterscheidet
in der tat
die leere der stille ist ferne

öffentlicher aushang 112
weder hier noch dort
bearbeitet vom brunnenfrosch »Kleiner Tellerrand«

das beispiel

Im gras am rand eines munteren gebirgsbächleins, von träumen ferner ziele beflügelt, übermütig glucksend dahineilend, steht hoch aufgerichtet ein murmeltier, ihm langsam entgegenkommend eine meeresschildkröte.

"Wohin des weges, unbekannte freundin?" Doch im stillen sich fragend, "was mag die fremde nur hierher verschlagen haben?"
Diese, langsam näher gekommen, erwidert etwas unsicher, "mein gruß zurück, ja, ich suche das murmeltier."
"So so, welches murmeltier denn, wir sind nicht wenige hier."
"Es besuchte mich, erst ein paar tage ist das her, unten am meer, und meinte, der abschied wiege ihm schwer, so vieles, das von ihm sicher noch eine ganze weile zurückbliebe."
"Ach der, ja genau der, behauptet, er wäre von seiner letzten reise noch nicht wieder hier und ist dennoch da. Ist doch seltsam, nicht? Aber sieh´ selbst, du triffst ihn weiter oben nahe der quelle am felssturz."

Die meeresschildkröte, das letzte stück des weges auch noch geschafft, voller stolz kann sie endlich ihren freund begrüßen.
"Überraschung, mein bester, mit schönen grüßen vom meer."
"Meine gute freundin, ich erwartete deinen besuch, sind dir doch deine gedanken vorausgeeilt. Meine erinnerungen sind dagegen immer noch hierher unterwegs. Wir müssen uns wohl zeit lassen."
"Wie soll ich´s verstehen? Kann auch nicht lange verweilen, die höhe, wie du weißt."
"Macht doch nichts, deinen gedanken tut´s gut, noch eine weile zu bleiben, und sobald meine eintreffen, können beide sich in aller ruhe miteinander austauschen."
"Während ich wieder auf dem heimweg bin?"
"Und darüber hinaus, meine freundin. Habe ich dir doch erklärt, wie sich das mit dem reisen verhält."

gesang der grille Tritonus

anwesend und auch wieder nicht
realität und illusion
einen festen ort gibt es nicht
auch der polarstern steht nicht still
hin und her läuft im glaspalast
der wolfshund und jagt den mond

öffentlicher aushang 113
haben die alten da was verschwiegen?

bearbeitet und kommentiert
vom brunnenfrosch »Kleiner Tellerrand«

hinweis

In der herberge und dem gasthaus "zum falschen pfifferling" gehören die abende den forstarbeitern. Robuste und trinkfeste waldameisen, und so kreisen alsbald die bierkrüge. Auch anwesend der lehrer der waldschule, Erasmus, ein ameisenrüsselkäfer, von allen hoch geschätzt. Verteidigt er doch erfolgreich die waldarbeitergemeinde bei allen streitigkeiten mit der verwaltung des klösterlichen Vacanti, besitzer des waldes.
Heute gilt die neugierde vieler stammgäste der eintagsfliege Wu-wei, eine alte freundin des lehrers und zu besuch.

das beispiel

Der holzfäller Heduda, ein vorsichtige frage an Wu-wei: "Wie kommt eine eintagsfliege so über die runden und kann sagen ...", etwas unsicher blickt er hinüber zu Erasmus, " … also einfach so, zu sagen, tag für tag ein guter tag?"
Wu-wei: "Das ist die weisheit der alten, die vor uns waren."
"Haben sie dir da nicht auch was verschwiegen?"
"Das haben sie."
"Und ...", wieder blickt Heduda unschlüssig zu dem lehrer, der aber nickt ermutigend, "wie soll ich das wieder verstehen?"
Wu-wei: "Können wir mit einer handvoll sand erklären, wie unfassbar weit sich der meeresstrand erstreckt?"
Heduda blickt nachdenklich auf die leeren gläser. Er ruft den wirt:
"Patron, ich frage dich, die bierlachen auf dem tisch, geben die eine ahnung wie herrlich ein frisch gezapftes bier zischt? Zwei für meine beiden gelehrten freunde und ein drittes mir, auf meine kreide."

Wu-wei, aus ihrem gelehrten himmel ins tiefe gras gestürzt, sie weiß das sehr zu schätzen, desgleichen den wohlgemeinten trunk.

gesang der grille Tritonus

die sandkörner in einer hand
unerschlossen bleiben die welten
ungezählte durch die finger rinnen
die sanduhr misst nur eine zeit
so auch tag für tag um tag für tag
die huldigung des morgens
dem abend gilt sein dank

öffentlicher aushang 114
Osramus' angepasste wahrheit
bearbeitet und *kommentiert*
vom brunnenfrosch »Kleiner Tellerrand«

das beispiel

Ein gebirgstal, dem himmel näher als manche hinter ihnen versunkene gipfel, und vor ihnen richtet der wind düstere wolkentürme auf, als gelte es eine störrische herde unter aufsicht der umgebenden weißen häupter zu stellen. Die beiden pilger, Krätze, die kellerassel und der leuchtkäfer Osramus, schätzen sich glücklich, vor dem drohenden schneesturm in einem weltabgeschiedenen kloster schutz gefunden zu haben.

Kaum im refektorium platz genommen, schon fragt der vorsteher: "Sagt mir doch, was gibt es neues?"
Krätze: "Der wind pfeift es soeben ums gemäuer."
Vorsteher: "Der wind bläst aus westen, ihr beide kommt aus dem osten."
Ein erster blitz und anhaltendes donnergrollen aus der ferne lässt die zum mahl versammelten innehalten und lauschen.
Krätze, in demütiger verbeugung, zu seinem gastgeber: "Aus dem osten, herr vorsteher, der glockenklang des lichts hat uns einen sicheren weg gewiesen."
"Der bltzschlag des lichts ist kein sicherer wegbegleiter. Über die von launischem wetter belagerte passhöhe hat vor euch noch nie ein pilger seinen weg zu uns gefunden. Doch sagt, was gibt es neues?"
Osramus spürt die spannnung, erstrahlt in mildem leuchten, "ob west, ost, süd oder nord, irren wir erst einmal durch tiefes gras, dann narrt uns jede frage."

Die kellerassel Krätze scheint heute dünnhäutig aufgekratzt. Osramus' bescheidenes licht schafft diesmal klarheit. Sperre, wer will da noch was draufsetzen?

gesang der grille Tritonus

neuigkeiten im hier und jetzt
erinnerungen oder angepasste wahrheiten
abgeschiedenheit ist nähe
nähe unterscheidet sich nicht von abgeschiedenheit
noch ist abgeschiedenheit von nähe unterscheidbar
in der tat
nähe ist abgeschiedenheit

öffentlicher aushang 115
the proof of the pudding …
bearbeitet vom brunnenfrosch »Kleiner Tellerrand«

hinweis

Durch einen vermisstenaushang in seiner dienststelle, zur fandung nach einer "entlaufenen" gefährlichen pflanze, ist Piedplat, der dickkopffliege und streifenpolizist, längst bekannt, dass es sich um die ihm zugelaufene orchidee handeln muss, die immer noch als flüchtig gilt und strafrechtlich gesucht wird. Ein gärtner des Vacanti hat die züchtung einer pflanzenart gestanden, die leidenschaftlich dem verzehr und der löschung von tinten- und druckerschwärze zugetan ist. Alle ämter und verwaltungen sind gewarnt.

das beispiel

Piedplat: "Ein für allemal, wurzeln weg von meinen romanen, sie auf geistige art zu genießen, davon verstehst du nichts."
"Im universum ist alles eine frage des stoffwechsels."
"Das lesen ausgenommen, schreib dir das hinter deinen blüten. Das ist eine frage des geschmacks, verstanden", erwidert der genervte Piedplat.
"Sag´ ich doch", beteuert seine hausgenossin.
"Verdreh mir nicht die worte. Bei dir ist zwischen blatt und blüte bis zu den wurzelspitzen leider kein verstand zwischengeschaltet."
"Wie oft soll ich dich daran erinnern, du kannst nicht wissen, wie es ist, eine orchidee zu sein und gib zu, wir streiten uns doch wie verständige leute."
"Womöglich halte ich nur selbstgespräche und sehe gespenster?"
"Dann blätter mal in dem neuen romanheft, das du letzte nacht auf dem küchentisch liegengelassen hast."
Piedplat greift hektisch nach dem schmöker: "Leere seiten. Das ist wieder mal dein gefräßiges werk."
"Bitte beachte, genau eine seite vor dem eingeknickten eselsohr habe ich meinen appetit gezügelt, so kannst du unbesorgt zu ende lesen. Im universum gibt's auch kooperation."

gesang der grille Tritonus

labend sollen sie schon sein, die künste
vorteil für den magen, dem herzen nahe
näher als der kopf
doch gute sitte ist's bei tisch,
in fragen des geschmacks kopf und
magen in bester eintracht speisen zu lassen

öffentlicher aushang 116
kannst du rückwärts gehen?
bearbeitet und kommentiert
vom brunnenfrosch »Kleiner Tellerrand«

das beispiel

"Das meer liegt da hinter den dünen, nicht zu verfehlen, mächtig breit."
So erreicht das murmeltier ein im strand eingebettetes felsiges ufer, bei flut vom meer umspült, Um das gestein hebt und senkt sich gemächlich eine sanfte dünung.
"Wie ruhig das meer atmet", ruft das murmeltier beeindruckt und lauscht dem in hohlräumen gluckernden wasser, was sich anhört als plaudere das meer mit jemandem.
"Wohl fremd hier?" meldet sich ein einsiedlerkrebs.
"Ja, ich suche meine freundin, die meeresschildkröte."
"Kannst du rückwärts gehen?" Der krebs macht es vor.
"Ist das nötig?"
"Ich denke wohl. Willst du einer gefahr einfach den rücken zukehren?"
"Die suche ich nicht. Wer zeigt mir den weg zur meeresschildkröte?"
"Ja ich natürlich."
"Oh ja, danke."
"Kannst du rückwärts gehen?" Damit zieht der einsiedlerkrebs sich in die dunkelheit einer im tieferen wasser gelegenen felsnische zurück. Im glucksen des wassers zwischen dem gestein bleibt dies dem murmeltier dennoch ein tröstliches geraune, eine ermutigende botschaft:
"Wu-wei, ihr werdet euch nicht verfehlen."
Das murmeltier macht kehrt, anderweitig zu suchen.
"Sehe ich recht, du hast mich also gefunden", rief von weitem die langsam ihm entgegenkommende meeresschildkröte.

Dies ließe nun vermuten, der einsiedlerkrebs Hieronymus wäre zu streichen aufgelegt, doch in seinem freudlosen zwischenreich ist er weder hier noch dort.. Mein beifall gilt hier der unbeirrbaren freundschaft, einem festen band, das sicher geleitet.

gesang der grille Tritonus

gebirgshöhen und meerestiefen
den einen aussicht, den anderen weitsicht
wem gilt der brunnenrandhorizont?
Des grillengesangs bescheidene stimmen
das raunen der elemente, ohne dem
fehlte der welt ihr zeitmaß

öffentlicher aushang 117
Osramus geht ein licht auf
bearbeitet vom brunnenfrosch »Kleiner Tellerrand«

das beispiel

Johann Custos der feuerkäfer, aller Vacanti-ämter längst entledigt, ein wunschlos genügsamer eremit hoch oben in seiner klause im geäst eines korallenbaumes, von den adepten des instituts wegen seiner schroffen art gemieden, ihm nur recht, doch heute stellt sich ein besucher ein. Die pilgernde kellerassel Krätze lässt sich nicht so leicht entmutigen. Ein weiteres mal nähert sie sich dem meister, unverdrossen, diesmal in begleitung eines treuen freundes, des leuchtkäfers Osramus. Beide verharren in verbeugung vor dem sitz des alten.

Der eremit zögert nicht: "Lassen wir das, sag mir nur, dürftest du nicht aus erfahrung meine frage ahnen, mir als erstes zu erklären, woher du heute des weges kommst?"
"Mein mentor Wu-wei, die eintagsfliege, wies mir einst weg und richtung, Ein ziel nannte er nicht. Mir schien es hier richtig zu sein. Warum nicht doch besser vor den toren des Vacanti, dort im gasthaus »zum falschen pfifferling«, das frage ich mich jetzt selbst."
Der purpurrote feuerkäfer schweigt.
Mit einer erneuten verbeugung will Krätze sich verabschieden. Ohne jegliche vorwarnung stößt Johann Custos ihn vom korallenast, blickt ihm nach, wie er unten ins tiefe gras trudelt und ruft hinterher:
"Habe ich dich denn nach dem woher gefragt?"
Er seufzt, ein leises zwiegespräch mit sich: "Eigentlich müsste ich diesem mutigen wanderer dort unten gesellschaft leisten."
Der leuchtkäfer Osramus hat das nicht überhört. Unverzugs bringt er den vornüber gebeugten mit einem kleinen schubs aus dem sowieso schon labilen gleichgewicht, und so landet dieser ebenfalls im tiefen gras am fuß des korallenbaums.

gesang der grille Tritonus

gedacht aber nicht getan
gesagt aber nicht gemeint
in der richtung des windes das feuer anblasen
vorsätzlich dem dieb die leiter hingestellt
der klopft höflich an die tür

öffentlicher aushang 118
schlaflos im steinigen bett
bearbeitet vom brunnenfrosch »Kleiner Tellerrand«

das beispiel

Ein reiher, auf ausgedehntem flug, ein gebirge durchquerend, findet in einem tal schutz für die nacht und rastet am ufer eines flusses, dessen unruhiges geraune sich nach und nach zu einer deutlich vernehmbaren klage steigert: "Herzloses tal, mir nur ein steinernes bett bereiten, und die weichen wiesen für den abendwind."

"Wann hört das endlich mal auf", grummelt das im schlaf gestörte schilfrohr. Der reiher versucht es mit tröstenden worten: "Lieber fluss, gräme dich nicht, bedenke doch, tagaus tagein in deinem bett, wer kann sich das schon leisten? Dein name ist ohne substanz, schall und rauch."
"Was redet dieser fremde vogel da", empört sich der fluss, "ich leite das wasser zum meer, ein gewichtiges unterfangen."
"Bleiben sie ganz entspannt, das wasser findet seinen weg von alleine", versucht der reiher den fluss zu besänftigen.
Wieder das schilfrohr: "Jetzt haben wir den salat, Dieser junge spund von fluss, ein unerfahrener wichtigtuer."
Der reiher ahnt, hier herrscht ein dauerzwist.
Das schilfrohr ist nicht mehr zu bremsen: "Du naseweis mit deinen wassern, hast du dir jemals gedanken darüber gemacht, wie es denen am meer ergehen wird?"
Der reiher bereut seine einmischung.
Das schilfrohr beantwortet seine zuvor gestellte frage selbst: "In der innigen umarmung des euch empfangenden ozeans fahrt ihr in den ideenhimmel auf. Wie der reiher sagte, schall und rauch."
Greinend nimmt der fluss sein lamento wieder auf, doch die stimme klingt schwach, was wunder, so nahe am wasser gebaut, und versiegt alsbald in gleichmäßigem glucksen. Alle anderen finden ihren verdienten schlaf.

gesang der grille Tritonus

der maulwurf Platon weiß nichts von seiner blindheit
im glaspalast stürmt der wolfshund
treppauf treppab, jagt heulend den weißen mond
und auf Desolation Peak
Ray Smith übt sich im kopfstand
der füße fester grund im leeren
eine leichte last, das Sein der welt

öffentlicher aushang 119
freiheit der leere
bearbeitet vom brunnenfrosch »Kleiner Tellerrand«

das beispiel

Graf Compo von Asselfrei, nobilitierte kellerassel, mit equipage im gasthaus "zum falschen pfifferling" einquartiert, hat sich, mit der waldarbeiterameise Heduda als führer, in das nah gelegene Vacanti begeben. Für diesen besuch bescheiden gekleidet, wird der graf vom hausherrn Bel Nimra, einem prächtigen scharlachroten feuerkäfer, in der eingangshalle begrüßt.

Linkisch und übertrieben verbeugt sich die gräfliche kellerassel vor dem leiter des instituts. "Hochwürden, mich dürstet nach dem segen der rechten und wahren lehre."
Etwas abseits Heduda, darauf wartend, den zustehenden führerlohn ausgezahlt zu bekommen. Bel Nimra führt den grafen vor eine der zwei großen porzellanvasen, am treppenaufgang beidseitg aufgestellt, und bittet seinen gast, laut hörbar dagegen zu klopfen.
"Klingt sie nicht verdächtig hohl?" fragt er seinen leicht irritierten gast.
"Jaaah, aber …"
"Da braucht's kein aber, zuviel leere ist nicht gut. Nahe am nichts, der verneinung der schöpfung, Verehrter graf, was lehrt und das?"
Graf Compo fällt es schwer, diesem gedanken zu folgen. Bel Nimra erwartet wohl auch keine antwort und fährt fort: "Die reichen haben ihren glauben in der truhe."
"Jaaah, aber …"
"Wie wunderschön klingelt es doch in einer vase, wenn goldmünzen hineinrieseln. Das erhebt die seele. Das ist doch ihr wunsch."
"Jaaah, aber, ihr segen … "
"Das geläut für die himmelfahrt der seele. Sehen sie nur ihren begleiter," beide blicken zu dem abseits stehenden Heduda, "ich sage ihnen, fröhliche armut ist ohne gut."
Heduda, erst verlegen, lässt seinen gedanken freien lauf: "Ich bitte herrn grafen mich noch zu entlohnen, mein himmelreich liegt im f*alschen pfifferling*, Das klingeln ihrer goldmünzen in der vase wird mich von meiner trockenen kehle nicht erlösen."

gesang der grille Tritonus

lehre ist leere
leere unterscheidet sich nicht von lehre
noch dass sich lehre von leere unterscheidet
in der tat, leere ist lehre

öffentlicher aushang 120
ombres chinoises
bearbeitet vom brunnenfrosch »Kleiner Tellerrand«

das beispiel

Einem schatten, untadelig, pflichtbewusst und welterfahren, kommen bedenken, er könnte im dienst eines hochstaplers stehen, vermutlich ein schatten gleich ihm, doch dieser aufrecht gehend einem lebendigem wesen zu gleichen versucht. Er bringt dies nun zur sprache:

"Wenn's wahr ist, was ich annehme, das wär' betrug an uns selbst, uns schatten ist nicht erlaubt, unseresgleichen zu dienen."
Der aufrechte schatten hat sich umgedreht, und blickt den schatten hinter sich an: "Sie haben ja so recht. Ich unglückliche bin tatsächlich nur mehr ein schatten meiner selbst."
"Keine nebulöse ausrede, konkreter bitte."
Der stehende schatten senkt den kopf wie unter einer last.
"Ich wurde einst in den augen aller als blendend überirdisch schöne schauspielerin angehimmelt, keine rolle, in der ich mich nicht neu erfand, jede stand mir bestens zu gesicht."
"Wo viel licht ist, bekommen wir schatten gleichviel zu tun."
"Von einer identität häutete ich mich in die nächste. Im glanz der bühne begann ich mein selbst zu verlieren. Dann, von der welt vergessen, ein sturz in unbestimmte leere."
"Sie glückliche, nun konnten sie wieder sie selbst sein, zu sich selbst zurückfinden."
"Sie spotten, auch mein schatten verweigerte sich mir, ich war zum schatten meiner selbst gewandelt."
"Warum so eilig ins schattendasein flüchten. Den fluss Lethe werden sie noch früh genug überqueren. In jene schattenwelt bleibt mir wiederum der eintritt verweigert. Also sie sehen, wir schulden uns nichts."

gesang der grille Tritonus

bretter, die die welt bedeuten?
living on stage
the world in a frame
the world in a mirror
sie sagt
ich spiegele mich, also bin ich
same old story
the medium is the message
es lügt der schein
es trügt der spiegel

öffentlicher aushang 121
good old days
bearbeitet und *kommentiert*
vom brunnenfrosch »Kleiner Tellerrand«

das beispiel

Der feuerkäfer Johann Custos, in stiller klausur hoch oben auf seinem korallenbaum verweilend, bekommt besuch, diesmal kein übermütiger disputierfreudiger pilger, den er mit listigem vergnügen unversehens hinunter ins tiefe gras stürzen könnte, statt dessen steht eine stolze waffenfliege in metallisch grünglänzender uniform vor ihm, und wie sich herausstellt, ein studienfreund gemeinsamer zeiten an der berühmten Nonsobre.
"Johann, dich hier vor mir zu sehen, dein gleichmut wie eh und je, in deinem orangenen flügelkleid, goldglanz des bescheidenen, würde ich sagen, augenblicklich erinnerst du mich an manche glorreiche gute alte tage."
"So, mein freund, wie alt sind sie denn?"
"Alt genug um gut zu sein."
"Das klingt als zögest du deine erinnerungen auf flaschen, wie wein, ist dir die gegenwart, der augenblick so wenig genießbar?"
"Aber du erinnerst dich doch, was hatten wir noch für träume."
"Deine waren erfüllt vom glorienschein des ruhms, wohl wahr, und zwar keineswegs das blatt vom lorbeerkranz des poeten."
"Dem namen verpflichtet, ich bin eine waffenfliege."
"Dem stolz dürfte die dünne luft hier oben nicht gut tun, mein freund", er gibt seinem besucher unversehens einen leichten schubs, ausreichend das gleichgewicht zu verlieren, ein tiefer fall ins gras, ein stürzender stern mit einem schweif. Von oben nachgerufene worte:
"Tag für tag ist ein guter tag, die triumphe von gestern oder morgen, ein allzu schweres gepäck für's gegenwärtig sein."

Dieses beispiel spricht auch den klausner des korallenbaums nicht gerade frei von trug und narrheit.

gesang der grille Tritonus

wo das leben sich ereignet
in einander gefaltete momente
die toten dürften es wissen
wir lebende träumen
im spiegel das Ich, gaukelei
vom ersten schrei zum letzten atemzug
ei-ner-lei

öffentlicher aushang 122
ein verlorener horizont
bearbeitet und *kommentiert*
vom brunnenfrosch »Kleiner Tellerrand«

das beispiel

Der meereshorizont hatte seine zwei pilgernden freunde, Krätze, die kellerassel, und Osramus, den leuchtkäfer, auf seinen schultern über das gebirge getragen. Nun bedanken sich beide artig für diese hilfe.

"Keine ursache, ich wollte immer schon mal sehen was die horizonte im gebirge so treiben. Doch mit der verwandtschaft ist's nicht weit her, von unstetem geist, gaukeln herum, wie der hase läuft, biegen hier ab, zeigen sich dort, sich sogleich wieder dem blick entziehend."

Betreten schweigen die beiden freunde, möchten sich nicht in familiäre konflikte einmischen.

"Ihr seid doch weitgereist und könnt's bestätigen, bin ich nicht der beweis dafür, dass die welt rund ist, von stetiger krümmung, die sich in einem kreis schließen muss? Mit ausdauer kämt auch ihr reisende irgendwann wieder an den selben ort zurück."

"Ob die zeit uns dazu reichte? Manche sagen, die zeit habe ein ende", gab Osramus zu bedenken.

Krätzes freund haben die gedanken ihres helfers in widersprüche nicht mehr fassbarer dimensionen entführt.

"Das hat sie", erwidert der meereshorizont, "der heutige tag ist jünger als der gestrige, da wir aufgebrochen sind, und der wiederum war schon jünger ist als der vorgestrige …."

"Stimmt, aber …"

"… aber so werden mit der zeit die tage immer jünger, nun sagt mir, ihr beiden, wie kann das gut gehen?"

Die anstehende rückkehr zur horizontalen langeweile scheint dem meereshorizont nun arg auf's gemüt zu drücken.

"Oh jeh, heißt das, bis dass der jüngste tag noch ungeboren ist?" so Krätzes vorsichtige, kleinlaute frage.

"Ach, mir schwirrt der kopf, muss mich hinlegen, macht's gut, ihr beiden", und macht sich auf den weg zurück zum ozean.

"Danke und gute besserung" ruft Osramus ihm nach.

gesang der grille Tritonus

horizonte zerbröseln   die sonnen eingerollt
hinter jedem schritt   versinkt ein tag
eingegangen in   ungeborene zeit

öffentlicher aushang 107
Piedplat und der stoff der träume

bearbeitet und kommentiert
vom brunnenfrosch »Kleiner Tellerrand«

das beispiel

Die dickkopffliege Piedplat, ein streifenpolizist, hat soeben der, in seinem revier, dem Bois de Brume, ihm zugelaufenen seltsamen orichdeenpflanze, in einem mit guter gartenerde gefüllten tontopf verdünnte tinte zu trinken gegeben.

"Warum stellst du mir nicht einfach das tintenfass auf den tisch, oder lässt mich zeitung lesen ?" fragt die fremde.

Kleiner Tellerrand - *sollten wir uns diese dialoge eher als eine weise stummer gedankenübertragung vorstellen* ?

"Ich möchte nicht dass du herumtaperst, in meinen romanen blätterst, zumindest nicht bevor ich sie selbst gelesen habe."

"Aber sie sind nahrhaft und von besonderem geschmack."

"So wie ich am tisch esse, so nimmst du bitte deine malzeiten in deinem topf ein, und gedrucktes naschen gibt es nicht."

"Was immer dir das gedruckte bedeutet, mich nährt es."

"Du bist nur auf die druckerschwärze aus. Aber deine tintenration ist mehr als großzügig. Und überhaupt, deine ernährung, ist das pflanzenart - frage ich dich ?"

"Ich bin nicht du, und du weißt nicht wie es ist ich zu sein."

Kleiner Tellerrand – *zu behaupten, alles sei subjektiv, wie paradox, kann das denn zugleich objektiv gültig sein* ?

Piedplat: "Du hast zu oft in der bibliothek des Vacanti heimlich in den bücherregalen herumgestöbert und dir dabei ganz schön den magen verdorben."

gesang der grille Tritonus

How does a table know how it is
to be a dog running free ?
When plants drag out their roots
walking´ round in a spooky manner,
when narrative becomes plain fiction
but thoughts still cast a light on reality
at it´s best - we´ll accept it:
"the willing suspension of disbelief" *

* James Taylor Coleridge

Der verfasser dieser »zwei mal elf« *beispiele*, wurde von den »gong'an« (öffentlichen aushängen) des »Bi-yän-lu« angeregt. Zwischen april 2016 und august 2019 von ihm im postkarten im format DIN-lang ohne absender verschickt worden, an etwas über neunzig adressaten. Die adressseiten wurden vom autor mit abbildungen aus dem archiv seiner tuschen und zeichnungen versehen, in der absicht, das ganze einer vorgefassten sinngebung noch ein stück weiter zu entziehen.

Der autor entschuldigt sich bei den einstigen empfängern dieser karten, sollte ihnen das unnötige kopfschmerzen bereitet haben. Er fühlte sich entlastet, als immerhin einer von ihnen, der schließlich nach längerer zeit von seiner urheberschaft ahnte, ihm gestand, er hätte die karten aus ratlosigkeit eine geraume zeit lang zügig entsorgt. Kann nur sagen, gut gehandelt, das, was wandelt, ist an keinen pfahl zu binden.

Die einhundert beispiele des »Bi-yän-lu« wurden in China von dem ch'an buddhistischen mönch Hsüä-dou (980–1052) gesammelt und mit gesängen bedacht. Diese sammlung wurde im weiteren von dem mönch Yüan-wu (1063–1135) in den jahren 1111 bis 1115 mit umfangreichen kommentaren versehen und erhielt den den titel:

»Meister Yüan-wu's Niederschrift von der Smaragdenen Felswand«
erstmals im jahr 1300 gedruckt.

Abbildungen
geriebene Tusche, getuschte Aquarell- und Gouache-Farben

seite 6   *solitary tree thriving on mindscape* (2016)
      Öl-Acryl Malkarton 230 g/m2   50 x 70 cm
seite 8   *under the waning moon* (0216)
      Öl-Acryl Malkarton 230 g/m2   73 x 64 cm
seite 10 *nächtliche straßenpflasteridylle* (2013)
      aus dem Album *Platons Irrtum*   23 x 33 cm
seite 12 *Cirque de Gavarnie* (2013)
      Öl-Acryl Malkarton 230 g/m2   64 x 96 cm
seite 14 *ein himmel voller regen* (2008)
      Torchon Aquarellpapier 375 g/m2   60 x 90 cm
seite 16 *cloudwatching turtle* (2015)
      Zeichenkarton 150 g/m2   29,5 x 21,5 cm
seite 18 *frustriertes schoßhündchen* (2016)
      Bleistiftzeichnung   41,5 x 48,5 cm
seite 20 *glanzstar und kleine wolke* (2017)
      Tagebuch Skizze   30 x 41,5 cm
seite 22 *les cieux se précipitent dans le vide* (2016)
      Chinapapier "Wenzhou" 30 g/m2   50 x 70 cm
seite 24 *behüteter gebirgssee* (2015)
      Toh-Japanpapier 37 g/m2   24,5 x 34 cm

seite 26 *florissant songe d´un vase* (2017)
          Chinapapier "Wenzhou" 30 g/m2   69 x 96 cm
seite 28 *schnabelfels* (2017)
          Chinapapier "Wenzhou" 30 g/m2   68 x 96 cm
seite 30 *am rand des pilzwaldes* (2017)
          Chinapapier "Wenzhou" 30 g/m2   68 x 96 cm
seite 32 *kürbisvogel* (2017)
          Toh-Japanpapier 37 g/m2   21 x 29,5 cm
seite 34 *tout prêt pour l´excursion en voilier* (2004)
          (Pierre Bonnard und sein Frau Marthe)
          Öl-Acryl Malkarton 230 g/m2   50 x 65 cm
seite 36 *möwenfelsen am meer* (2014)
          Chinapapier "Wenzhou" 30 g/m2   45 x 62 cm
seite 38 *painter's déjà vu* (2017)
          Chinapapier "Wenzhou" 30 g/m2   53 x 67 cm
seite 40 *dans une ténébreuse et profonde unité* (2016)
          Chinapapier "Wenzhou" 30 g/m2   40 x 60 cm
seite 42 *über die höhe des gebirgspasses* (2016)
          Öl-Acryl Malkarton 230 g/m2   48 x 68 cm
seite 44 *die mondin und die hyäne* (2005)
          Öl-Acryl Malkarton 230 g/m2   60 x 91 cm
seite 46 *don't tell anyone (no GPS)* (2019)
          Chinapapier "Wenzhou" 30 g/m2   68 x 96 cm
seite 48 *time chokes down whatever it is* (2018)   Bildausschnitt
          Chinapapier "Wenzhou" 30 g/m2   69 x 96 cm

Talks on Self Enquiry:

A collection of writings on Self Enquiry

(Atma Vichara)

according to the teaching of Ramana Maharshi
by Miles Wright

ed. by Gabriele Ebert

We start from 'I' and end in 'I'. But look for 'I' and 'I' is nowhere to be found.

INHALT

Foreword by the Editor 5
The Living Teacher 6
What is Atma Vichara? 9
Talks on Atma Vichara 13
Bibliography 87

FOREWORD BY THE EDITOR

This is a collection of writings by Miles Wright about Self Enquiry (Atma Vichara) as taught by Ramana Maharshi. They are mostly responses to questions asked by members on various yahoo-groups (Ramana Maharshi, Atma Vichara, The Sage of Arunachala and Acalayoga) from 2000 to 2007.

Before this groups have been deleted I managed to save the most important writings, or what I felt may be of interest for a later reading and study for my personal use. Amongst them many are on Atma Vichara and also deal with misconceptions, which still circulate. I feel these questions and answers may also be of great value for others, and with Miles' permission this collection can now be offered to the public.

Gabriele Ebert

Note: The painting on the cover is by Miles Wright. It says hRd (heart) and hrdaya kuhara madhye (in the centre of the cave of the Heart) in Sanskrit from Ramana's famous verse Ramana Gita 2.2.

THE LIVING TEACHER

"I have a living teacher. Many seekers do not." This is a subject which has been written about on numerous occasions. It seems pertinent to write about it again. I trust you will be patient when I say, without flippancy "I also have a "living" teacher, His name is Bhagavan Sri Ramana Maharshi."

The living versus dead controversy seems to be a fundamental misunderstanding of the philosophy of Sri Ramana Maharshi (certainly fundamental in my sadhana). If I could relate a little of my own sadhana regarding this.

When I was a child I came across the name of Ramana Maharshi in a book about yoga. While I began to practice hatha yoga, (with relative ease, and to the amusement of my parents) the name 'Ramana Maharshi' fascinated and seemed to permeate my entire being. In this small book there is only one paragraph about the Sage, but this one paragraph sufficed to leave an indelible mark:

"'Pursue the enquiry "Who am I?" relentlessly,' advised an Indian guru, Sri Ramana Maharshi. 'Analyse your entire personality. Try to find out where the I-thought begins. Go on with your meditations. Keep turning your attention within. One day the wheel of thought will slow down and an intuition will mysteriously arise. Follow that intuition, let your thinking stop and it will eventually lead you to the goal.'"

Interestingly, the book was called 'Teach Yourself Yoga' written by James Hewitt. While I read this single paragraph over and over again, I never knew, nor did I consider, that Ramana Maharshi was other than alive. Did it matter? As I was only 13 years of age, it was not possible to travel to see him, but I did give vague consideration to finding out where he lived with a view to visiting at some future date. Months later, as my small Yoga Library began to take shape, the realisation that he was in fact dead came about (this may have been after reading a Paul Brunton book). While initially problematic, I very quickly understood that the Teaching (as revealed in the paragraph above) was, in effect, Ramana Maharshi's core teaching. A few years later I contacted the Ashram and purchased Talks, and a few other publications. During this time the practice of Vichara became my primary sadhana. My fascination with Sanskrit and Yoga continued and I met various yogis and spiritual teachers of the time (early 70s) but none could offer anything remotely as effective, at hitting the Heart of the matter, as the above paragraph.

In the early years my practice was limited to a certain time and place, and pursued as a meditation. However fuelled by the conversations found in Talks, it soon developed into the primary occupation of mind and continued throughout the working day. This vivid teaching occupied my entire life.

Bhagavan Sri Ramana Maharshi is considered to be a jivanmukta (one who has attained freedom while living). So what is this confusion about 'living'?

A friend sent me a book, 'Surpassing Love and Grace'. In it Chadwick says, "The whole mistake is initial, in the interpretation they put on the word jivanmukta; or in what they think a jnani really is and how he functions. When it is found that a jivanmukta is already absorbed in the Infinite and that for him the apparent change he undergoes is no change at all, there should be no more misapprehensions. There is no further step for a jnani to take; he lost all sense of doership or association with a particular body when he finally knew himself to be a jnani. The physical death is only just a happening in the myriad strange happenings in maya. He was in no way limited to a body while it was functioning. It was there, one might almost say, for us. We needed something that we could see, somebody who could speak to us. Now we must get along without the comfort of the physical presence, but it does not mean Bhagavan has gone anywhere, indeed, as he said himself: 'Where could I go? I am always here.'" (p. 260)

For anyone requiring a 'physical' presence the Ashram remains and publishes books which reveal Ramana Maharshi's teachings. For those with a more esoteric inclination, Guru stands resplendent as the hill, Sri Arunachala. The most potent representation, however, is the practice of Vichara (Self-enquiry). To quote Chadwick again, "To what after all, did his spoken instructions amount? There is only one Self. You are that. Amplifying it slightly it becomes: there is nothing to do, nothing to seek. There is only false identification with limitation to discard and that is done by concentration on the eternal witness, the One behind all phenomena. Know who you are and there is no more to know." (p. 261) And this is also the instruction revealed (above), from day one, to the young lad reading his first book on Yoga.

From Talks; p. 434:

"D. : Sadguru is necessary to guide me to understand it.

M. : The Sadguru is within.

D. : I want a visible Guru.

M. : That visible Guru says that He is within.

D. : Can I throw myself at the mercy of the Sadguru?

M. : Yes. Instructions are necessary only so long as one has not surrendered oneself.

This is the Truth. Of that there is absolutely no doubt."

WHAT IS ATMA VICHARA?

A South Indian Sage advised, "Pursue the enquiry 'Who am I?' relentlessly! Seek out the root of your personality! Find out wherefrom the I-thought arises! Turn the mind within. With practice, the current of thoughts will slow down and an unerring intuition will be felt. Yield to that intuition, let your thinking stop, and it will pull you to the goal." (Hewitt: Teach yourself Yoga)

Vichara is often confused with meditation. Meditation however requires subject and object whereas Vichara eliminates the obsession with object completely.

Ramana Maharshi said, "Dhyana (meditation) is concentration on an object. It fulfils the purpose of keeping away diverse thoughts and fixing the mind on a single thought, which must also disappear before Realisation. But Realisation is nothing new to be acquired. It is already there, but obstructed by a screen of thoughts. All our attempts are directed for lifting this screen and then Realisation is revealed. If a true seeker is advised to meditate, many may go away satisfied with the advice. But someone among them may turn round and ask, 'Who am I to meditate on an object?' Such a one must be told to find the Self. That is the finality. That is Vichara." (Talk 390)

"Do not spread out the mind inquiring, 'Who may you be?' and 'Who is he?' Turn it inward questing, steadily, keenly, 'Who am I?'" (from Muruganar: Ramana Mandiram).

Atma Vichara (Self Enquiry) should not be considered as a mere yogic exercise to be done at certain times of the day and then forgotten until the next session, although that is certainly a valid way of introducing the mind to enquiry (but don't get lost in the introduction – how long does it take to shake hands?) Nor is Vichara a hobby, it is a way of life.

The Vichara method focusses on the meditator (the thinker) from the very outset. It is radical.

When, through Self Enquiry, brought about by intense practice, thoughts subside, there stands revealed an unbroken, eternal awareness, 'I'-'I'. It is not a watched awareness. Who is the subject that can claim such dualistic nonsense! The snake in the rope will never see the rope. 'I'-'I' is both herald and death knell.

"In the course of tracing ourselves back to our source, when all thoughts have vanished, there arises a throb from the Hridaya on the right, manifesting as 'Aham' 'Aham' 'I'-'I'. This is the sign that Pure Consciousness is beginning to reveal itself. But that is not the end in itself. Watch wherefrom this sphurana (throbbing) arises and wait attentively and continually for the revelation of the Self. Then comes the awareness, oneness of existence." (from a reply, approved by Bhagavan, which was sent to an English devotee; recorded in 'Moments Remembered' by V. Ganesan, p. 53)

"Thoughts must cease and reason disappear for 'I'-'I' to rise up and be felt. Feeling is the prime factor and not reason." (Talk 24)

"That which is does not even say 'I am'. For, does any doubt rise that 'I am not'." (from Talk 197)

Method

"When other thoughts arise, one should not pursue them, but should inquire: 'To whom do they arise?' It does not matter how many thoughts arise. As each thought arises, one should inquire with diligence, 'To whom has this thought arisen?'. The answer that would emerge would be 'To me'. Thereupon if one inquires 'Who am I?', the mind will go back to its source; and the thought that arose will become quiescent. With repeated practice in this manner, the mind will develop the skill to stay in its source." (from 'Who am I?')

Giving up the unreal claim on reality of the body and mind, the sadhaka must fix the mind on the individual 'I'-sense, which, although unreal, appears to be superimposed on the eternal substratum of the real Self. The question "Who am I?" is the means. If during this quest, the mind turns outwards again, predicating on this or that, the sadhaka should ask "To whom do these thoughts occur?" and thus move back to the primary quest "Who am I?" Sri K. Lakshmana Sarma says "Always and everywhere there are doorways for getting at the question 'Who am I?' By any one of these the seeker must again and again engage the mind in this Quest. The answer to this question is not an intellectual conclusion. The (proper) answer to it is only the Experience of the Real Self in the Supreme State, arising on the death of the ego, the questioner, named the 'individual self' (the soul)." (Sri Ramanaparavidyopanishad, 483 and 484; cf. 469-485)

The question "Who am I?" has no answer. No experience can answer it, for the Self is beyond experience... It has no answer in consciousness and, therefore, helps to go beyond consciousness.

"All I can say truly is: 'I am', all else is inference. But the inference has become a habit. Destroy all habits of thinking and seeing. The sense 'I am' is the manifestation of a deeper cause, which you may call self, God, reality or by any other name. The 'I am' is in the world; but it is the key which can open the door out of the world. The moon dancing on the water is seen in the water, but it is caused by the moon in the sky and not by the water." (Nisargadatta, in "I am That", p. 191)

To halt mindstuff, Self Enquiry (Vichara) is employed. Self Enquiry is becoming aware of aberrant thought and asking to whom it appears. This is it. Anything more is mindstuff. In this method, awareness of the absurdity of thought becomes heightened and, through practice, Self Enquiry cuts in more and more often.

"Q.: How will the mind become quiescent?

A.: By the inquiry 'Who am I?' The thought 'who am I?' will destroy all other thoughts, and like the stick used for stirring the burning pyre, it will itself in the end get destroyed. Then, there will arise Self-realization." (from Ramana Maharshi's 'Who Am I?')

Mind alone is the cause of bondage and liberation. A mind devoted to the world of objects is bound while a mind that is not devoted to the world of objects is liberated. Vichara reveals the ever present substrate upon which the mind relies. Since, in truth, there is no answer to the question, any answer the mind concocts provides fodder for further Enquiry. The path is therefore clear.

"If once Vichara takes root, the highest good has, for all practical purposes, been reached in this life. As long as Vichara is absent from a human being, the most desirable form of birth, so long is the tree of life barren and therefore useless. The only useful fruit of life is Vichara." (Tripura Rahasya, chapter 2)

Maharshi makes it very clear that there is no advanced method only maturation of the Vichara. Vichara is the direct method. "There is nothing more to be known than what you find in books. No secret technique. It is all an open secret, in this system." (Day by Day, 8.10.1946)

TALKS ON ATMA VICHARA

Ramana Maharshi

2.1.2000

When speaking to people I find that Vichara is often confused with meditation. Meditation however requires subject and object whereas Vichara eliminates the obsession with object completely.

As Ramana says in Talks [390] "The unreality is an obsession at present. Reality is our true nature... If a seeker is advised to meditate, many may go away satisfied with the advice. But someone among them may turn round and ask, 'Who am I to meditate on an object?' Such a one must be told to find the Self. That is the finality. That is Vichara... When spontaneous and natural it is Realisation."

4.1.2000

Ramana never taught a system of philosophy nor did he teach a 'method' for attaining enlightenment. His influence was that of a living presence of the Self. This presence is here and now. His Atma Vichara (Self Enquiry) is not a yogic exercise to be done at certain times of the day and then forgotten until the next session, although that is certainly a valid way of introducing the mind to enquiry, rather it is the very essence of a human life exploring its fullest potential.

How does Ramana's teaching influence our everyday life? Is there any influence? Does Atma Vichara kick in at times as a centering 'force'? How often does the ego run off during the day with its vehicle 'thought' way out of control? Dwelling on the past, looking to the future, living in any possible world it can, as long as it is not now? Do judgements and vendettas come fast and furious? Are we like the politician, elected on the policies that promise to help the people, who when elected hangs on for grim death whether or not policies are good or bad, the idea of doing good, per se, abandoned for "doing good as long as 'I' survive and it's good to 'me' too"? This survival of self, the ego, is in itself a fiction. Reflected light cannot radiate without the benefit of the source of that light.

6.1.2000

Devaraja Mudaliar has recounted that Bhagavan, in his younger days, used to go to the summit of Arunachala by a number of different routes, or even without a route, whenever he felt like it. Only the grass-cutters were aware of some of these routes.

He quotes the following story from Bhagavan.

"Sometimes people would come from Madras and other parts and, setting out to reach the top of the hill, would stray near Skandasramam. Finding me seated there, they would ask me for the route to the hill top. When I told them the route was to their right and turned northward, some would say, 'Do you know who we are and wherefrom we come?

We are from Madras. None of your tricks with us. The top is here straight above us and you want to lead us astray.' I used to keep quiet. They would try to climb in a straight line, and after a long time, they would return tired out, finding that all their efforts to reach the peak were in vain. Nearing me they would bow their heads in shame and go away, avoiding me."
(Mudaliar: Day by Day, 24.11.1945)

Here Bhagavan showed an easy and tested but seemingly circuitous route to the top but the advice was ignored. When talking of the spiritual path he offered the direct route and again his advice was often ignored.

14.1.2000

I have read a few rather bleak interpretations of 'predestination theory' recently which give enormous authority to destiny and the negation of any possible self-effort. When you turn to Ramana's proclamations on this subject all bleakness is dispelled.

"In order that the bonds of destiny
And all its kindred may at last be loosed,
And so that one may also be released
From the dread cycle of both birth and death,
This path than the others is far easier,
Therefore be still and keep a silent hold
On tongue and mind and body. That which is
The Self-effulgent will arise within.
This is the Supreme Experience. Fear will cease.
This is the boundless sea of Perfect Bliss!"

(Atma Vidya, from Collected Works, Rider 1975)

17.1.2000

The experience of the Self is indeed effortless. It is as it is. However once the truth of this becomes revealed it takes time to make it firm. Practice, and Bhagavan is clear that practice (effort) is necessary, ripens to reveal the knowledge of real Being.

22.1.2000

It is the universe in its diversity which is generally spoken of as reality. The pairs of opposites (dvandvas) vie for our attention. Good/bad, hot/cold, rich/poor, spiritual/material etc., we give our attention to all of these in order to make judgements on their relative merits. They are the all important opposites. All important because without them the universe as we 'know' it would collapse into Unity. This is how simple the task is. There is no mystery. Ramana Maharshi appeals to us to sacrifice everything for Truth. It is not that the mind of the jnani (Sage) and the mind of the ajnani (one who 'believes' enlightenment has yet to come) are different. This is simply thought.

The sum and substance of the enquiry "Who am I?" is "... to remain still." The wrong identification of Self with body and senses etc. is solved with this enquiry. This state of equilibrium is not unknown to us. To think it is, is again just thought.

samatvam yoga ucyate

It is said, "Equanimity is Yoga". [Bhagavad Gita II, 48]

Seer and seen, resolved as One.

29.1.2000

"What one fails to know by conversation extending to several years can be known in a trice in Silence, or in front of Silence – e.g. Dakshinamurti, and his four disciples. This is the highest and most effective language." (from Talk 246)

Many people have commented on, and attested to, the efficacy of Sri Ramana Maharshi's silence. Without words to activate the concept seeking mind there is instead the impetus to drive inwards to the source of the mind. Rather than hanging meaning on arbitrary words, the mind, devoid of outgoing, active content, finds the space to deliberately seek its source. This is called Satsanga, 'association with Being'. Whether in the presence of one who has realised the Self (perhaps the most common usage of the term), or in the mental presence of that One, the effect is the same. The gross medium of language is bypassed and the root of all thought, the primary 'I'-thought, is stopped in its tracks. With no thought arising there is no need for language. Neither human language nor thought are self-existent. In absence of thought universal silence spontaneously arises, or rather remains as it is, as the pure essence of speech. This is the Eternal Verbum, Sabda Brahman, Self.

Punyaraja says in his commentary on the Vakyapadiya: "The aspirant reaches the essence of speech, the Pure Verbum, which lies beyond the vital plane, by withdrawing his mind from external objects and fixing it upon his internal nature. This entails the dissolution of the temporal sequence of thought-activity. The purification of the Verbum (the eternal light of consciousness which ever shines within the subject) results from this and the aspirant enters into it having severed all ties with the material objective plane. This leads him to the attainment of the internal light and, freed from all bonds and limitations he becomes identical with the Supreme Light – the Eternal Word Principle – the undying and undecaying Spirit, called Sabdabrahman or the Word Absolute." (quoted in Sastri; 1959)

23.2.2000

A man was going through the forest when he was ambushed by an enemy and shot with a poisoned arrow. One of his kin stumbled upon him and raised the alarm and soon others arrived with antidotes to the poison. As they attempted to pull the arrow prior to applying the healing ointment the man prevented them and began to ask various questions such as, "You must find out for me: Who was that enemy? What was his family? Was he tall? What colour was his hair? What kind of bow did he use? What was the arrow made of? etc..." When it was suggested that the questions were irrelevant in the present situation and that without application of the healing herbs he would die he just continued to prevent treatment intent on gathering maximum information. Needless to say... the cure was not effective. [Buddhist parable of the poisoned arrow]

On the spiritual path this is exactly what we do. Having been told that Self Enquiry cuts directly to the source we still ask... "Who is the Creator? Why did he create? Why am I subjected to suffering? What is karma? Why do I make no progress? etc..." ad infinitum.

23.2.2000

"Yogananda: Why does God permit suffering in the world? Should He not with His omnipotence do away with it at one stroke and ordain the universal realisation of God?

Maharshi: Suffering is the way for Realisation of God.

Yogananda: Should He not ordain it differently?

Maharshi: It is the way.

Yogananda: Are Yoga, religion, etc., antidotes to suffering?

Maharshi: They help you to overcome suffering.

Yogananda: Why should there be suffering?

Maharshi: Who suffers? What is suffering?

No answer! Finally the Yogi rose up, prayed for Sri Bhagavan's blessings for his own work and expressed great regret for his hasty return. He looked very sincere and devoted and even emotional." (from Talk 107)

The arising of suffering gives impetus to the desire for happiness. This in turn brings about the successful quest of the Self. Suffering is due to the false notion 'I-am-the-body.' Jnanam (knowledge of the Self) is getting rid of this idea.

21.3.2000

>*I have been learning about Ramana Maharshi for the last ten years. During the last year I have started an active practice. The practice includes about one hour a day (20 minutes 3 times per day) in seated meditation focused on self-inquiry. As this meditation deepened, the inquiry extends to the rest of my activities.*<

Atma Vichara leads to the source of the ego. There the ego disappears. Remaining as that source the ego no longer arises. And as you suggest it goes on throughout all activities; walking, driving, eating etc.

22.3.2000

>*As I understand his [Ramana's] Self-Realization story, this Self Enquiry is what brought him to the realization. Did he ever actually say that? If he did, could you give a citation? He probably believed that early in his career.*<

Sri Bhagavan has said on many occasions that his great death-experience was essentially a questioning (Vichara) of whether the 'I' died with the death of the body. He also said quite categorically that this was not an act of reasoning but a flash of true perception. (cf. Mahadevan; 1977, Talks; 1955/1978, Osborne; 1959 (this is a truly excellent account) etc.) This was a 'direct experience' which he said never left him, not a 'probable belief early in his career'. His teaching never changed or developed. Why would it?

>*To clear up the ignorance as to who we really are Ramana again and again recommended Self Enquiry. He recommended many things, among them Self Enquiry. Since Self*

Enquiry was supposedly designed for the more educated and intelligent of his devotees, educated Westerners want to believe that Self Enquiry is the correct path for themselves. What is the evidence that Self Enquiry has 'worked' for anyone, as opposed to, say, japa or bhakti?<

Sri Bhagavan spoke on all sorts of paths according to the questions of the people who visited. His nearest devotees however are clear that Self Enquiry was the mainstay. For this we only have to look at the work of Sri Muruganar, the poet-devotee par excellence: "Do not spread out the mind inquiring 'Who may you be?' and 'Who is he?' Turn it inward questing steadily, keenly, 'Who am I?'"(from Ramana Mandiram)

And from Sri Bhagavan Himself in the last prose piece He wrote, 'Who am I?' prior to only responding verbally to enquiries. "... in order to realize that inherent and untainted happiness, which indeed he daily experiences when the mind is subdued in sleep, it is essential that he should know himself. For obtaining such knowledge the enquiry 'Who am I?' in quest of the Self is the best means."

21.3.2000

>You say: "There is no two – only God's will is acting through his manifestations." Sounds like two to me! Or maybe many! My understanding is that Ramana taught that God really does exist (even as the supreme creator of the universe). But, he taught further that such a premise is only true from the relative point of view – and is only maintained by those who have not realized the truth of the matter (those who believe in the reality of individual souls). God is the last form to go – not another form to be realized, thereby establishing the duality of God and his manifestations.<

Yes, as long as the individual is there to worship God so long do God and devotee exist independently. Unconditional surrender to the higher power or holding on to the root thought 'I' are the only two ways for realisation. (cf. Talk 321): ["If one surrenders oneself there will be no one to ask questions or to be thought of. Either the thoughts are eliminated by holding on to the root-thought 'I' or one surrenders oneself unconditionally to the Higher Power. These are the only two ways for Realisation."]

22.3.2000

Indeed Self Enquiry is the worthwhile pursuit. Engaging in polemics is a waste of time. If you practice Self Enquiry eventually it is found to be both the path and the goal.

Please continue to talk of spiritual practice if you are so moved. There are various ways to practice Self Enquiry which many would discuss.

22.3.2000

>*Thank you for the comment. I appreciate it. Of course what you say is known by mind, (showing again the almost useless nature of cognitive understanding when it comes to actual spiritual processes). As I practice I look for ways to bring this mere cognitive understanding into my experience and deep knowledge.<*

As Bhagavan has said: "In the union of the individual with the Supreme, the Supreme is hearsay and the individual directly experienced. You can make use only of direct experience; therefore look who you are." (from Talk 332)

>*One thing I have found about inquiry is that there are a lot of different angles of view. And for me it helps to look at ego-I from different viewpoints. It is like one dissolves a little ego here, some there, etc. I do this in a variety of life settings and situations, not just seated mediation (though this seated meditation is an important underpinning of my practice).<*

Indeed!! And the various ways to attain Self-realisation are exactly what Bhagavan discussed. Ultimately, of course, it is only the source of the 'I'-thought which needs attention. To get there the monkey-mind likes to leap through different branches.

29.3.2000

Self Enquiry is clinging to the first thought 'I', which must appear before the myriad others which fill the mind, holding on to this 'I'-thought and questioning 'who/what it is' is the practice.

A Part of 'Who am I?' is quoted below.

"10. How will the mind become quiescent?

By the inquiry 'Who am I?'. The thought 'who am I?' will destroy all other thoughts, and like the stick used for stirring the burning pyre, it will itself in the end get destroyed. Then, there will arise Self-realization.

11. What is the means for constantly holding on to the thought 'Who am I?'

When other thoughts arise, one should not pursue them, but should inquire: 'To whom do they arise?' It does not matter how many thoughts arise. As each thought arises, one should inquire with diligence, 'To whom has this thought arisen?' The answer that would emerge would be 'To me'. Thereupon if one inquires 'Who am I?', the mind will go back to its source; and the thought that arose will become quiescent. With repeated practice in this manner, the mind will develop the skill to stay in its source.

When the mind that is subtle goes out through the brain and the sense-organs, the gross names and forms appear; when it stays in the Heart, the names and forms disappear. Not letting the mind go out, but retaining it in the Heart is what is called 'inwardness' (antar-mukha). Letting the mind go out of the Heart is known as 'externalisation' (bahir-mukha). Thus, when the mind stays in the Heart, the 'I' which is the source of all thoughts will go, and the Self which ever exists will shine. Whatever one does, one should do without the egoity 'I'. If one acts in that way, all will appear as of the nature of Siva (God)." (from the book 'Who am I?')

Self Enquiry is not a meditation practice performed at certain times of the day. Although initially that may be the way one performs it. If the enquiry is persisted with throughout the day it will continue in sleep also. (This inevitably happens.)

Some have said that it is a mere mantra-like repetition. It is not. The purpose of Self Enquiry is to focus all attention, the entire mind, on its source. The result is Self-awareness. When the mind wanders Self Enquiry pulls it back to its source. That source is the Self.

Hope this helps. If not please say.

30.3.2000 "Who am I?"

It is analogous to a koan, in that as long as an answer appears the question will continue to be asked. The pull from within becomes intense through Self Enquiry.

However if Enquiry is a matter of saying, "now I'll do five minutes of Enquiry, then I'll watch the television, then I'll have time to go to the pub," then I wouldn't hold my breath waiting for whatever one might think one was waiting for to happen.

When Enquiry is first in your life then everything falls into place. The Self is the sole constant.

With persistence in the enquiry "Who am I?" all other thoughts are destroyed... And in the end the 'I'-thought itself is destroyed leaving the non-dual Self, resplendent as ever. One day something will happen.

The theoretical side is what one reads about, hears about in books or from the sages. This is where we gain intellectual conviction of the truth. And this in itself is important.

The Enquiry, while it may be a mental activity (intellectual) initially, becomes a subjective experience of 'I'. This experience in turn falls away when identification with objects through thoughts disappears. We start from 'I' and end in 'I'. But look for 'I' and 'I' is nowhere to be found.

There is no answer to the question, "Who am I?" It is 'Being' without qualification.

10.4.2000 Method

The aim is indeed the same, i.e. atmanishta [abiding in the Self] – to be fixed as the Self. In meditation with mind fixed on one thought all other thoughts are kept away. This is an excellent method for strengthening the mind which has a weakness for continual, random thoughts.

Practice of that method leads to Atma Vichara – Self Enquiry. When random thoughts are eliminated there still remains the meditator and the object of meditation. Then the meditator merges himself in the source. Ramana's method focusses on the meditator (the thinker) from the beginning. Ultimately that is what has to happen, a turning of attention on the one who thinks he is meditating.

Atma Vichara is a constant as long as the enquirer considers him/herself separate from enquiry. It does not have to be performed in a certain posture, for/at a certain time, or in a certain place. It is a continual process, while at work and while at play.

>*It seems to me that Ramana isn't particularly pointing to consciousness or even subjectivity here as an answer, nor a way to disidentify with or slow down the flow of thoughts. Rather I think he is advising a sort of active meditation on*

the sense or feeling of 'I'. When I say 'I' I mean something by that, although I couldn't exactly say what. I don't really mean consciousness or a kind of abstract subjectivity. I think the idea is to let oneself be pulled into the enquiry into what we mean by 'I'. Any comments? Can someone put this in better words?<

In a conversation Ramana points to the statements referring to the 'I'. "Who is the 'I' who says 'I' do not know?" Is it the real 'I' or the false 'I'? The 'I' who says "I am not realised" or "I do not know" is an impostor. When Ramana responds "Who was born?" he attempts again to point to the futility of this 'I'-thought, because what is born must also die. Realisation is not something to be gained anew. It is eternal. There is neither birth nor death for the Self.

Seeking the source of the 'I', however, *is* death for the 'I'. Then you will be only what you are, absolute being.

On another occasion Sri Ramana said to Swami Abhishiktananda: "Do not meditate – be! Do not think that you are – be! Don't think about being – you are!" [Abhishiktananda: Secrets, p. 73]

16.4.4.2000

>*Could you, or anyone, say something about the 'I'-'I' that Ramana sometimes talks about. I don't have a quote handy, but if you don't know what I'm referring to I can look one up.*<

In Talk 266 Sri Ramana says, "The real Self is the infinite 'I'-'I', i.e. 'I' is perfection. It is eternal. It has no origin and no end. The other 'I' is born and also dies. It is impermanent. See to whom are the changing thoughts. They will be found to arise after the 'I'-thought. Hold the 'I'-thought. They subside. Trace back the source of the 'I'-thought. The Self alone will remain."

'I'-'I' is the reality. For this 'I'-'I' to be felt, thoughts must cease and reason disappear. It has been noted that this is initially 'felt' as a throb on the right side of the chest. 'I'-'I', 'I'-'I'. This centre is the Hridaya [spiritual Heart], which Sri Ramana has revealed as the seat of Pure Consciousness in the body. This is the seat from which all experiences of the objective reality arise. Thoughts cannot enter here. The 'I'-thought is stopped dead in its tracks.

When the source of this throbbing is attentively observed there is revelation of the Self. To attain this through meditation or enquiry is to revel in unalloyed Bliss.

2.5.2000

>*Self Enquiry is not focussing on the meditator but to enquire whether there is a meditator.*<

Yes indeed, this is so. However while there is the belief that there is someone who meditates, directing the mind towards that meditator is the beginning of the quest. As Ramana says in Talk 580; "The ego must be held in order to get rid of it. Hold it first and the rest will be easy."

4.5.2000

>*Now if I understand Ramana correctly Self Enquiry is the direct method.*<

Yes.

>*However if we have to sit in meditation, get hold of the ego and then what kill it? The next question is how do I hold the ego? As an object of meditation? Is ego an object to be hold?*<

Who is it who would hold the ego? This is the point.

The ego is destroyed by seeking its identity. To try to hold it, you must first find it. This is the quest. "Because the ego is no entity it will automatically vanish and Reality will shine forth by itself. This is the direct method. ... The quest 'Who am I?' is the axe with which to cut of the ego." (from Talk 146)

30.11.2000

This, 'I-I', is the constant japa (or 'ajapa' – unspoken chant, i.e. effortless) of the Self in the Heart. It is never ceasing and eternally uncaused. Sri Bhagavan has mentioned (in various places) that if it appears in the body it does so in the Heart (Hridaya) on the right side of the chest. Yes, it can be observed during Self Enquiry. Bhagavan is careful to explain however, that this does not mean that the Self resides in the body. Rather the whole cosmos resides in the Heart. At the beginning of Talks, Bhagavan states... "the physical organ is on the left; that is not denied. But the Heart of which I speak is non-physical and is only on the right side. It is my experience, no authority is required by me. Still you can find confirmation in a Malayalam Ayurvedic book and in 'Sita Upanishad'"; and he produced the quotation (mantra) from the latter and repeated the text (sloka) from the former. (Talk 4)

It is also stated in Talks that... "Brahman is the Heart", "the Self is the Heart." Again Bhagavan says that "there is no one who even for a trice fails to experience the Self."

4.12.2000

I came across a more pertinent reference to this 'throbbing' from the seat of consciousness (Hridaya) today. It is taken from the reply to an enquiry sent to an English devotee by Sri T. K. Sundaresa Iyer. The reply was approved by Bhagavan. It appears in 'Moments Remembered', p. 53.

"In the course of tracing ourselves back to our source, when all thoughts have vanished, there arises a throb from the Hridaya on the right, manifesting as 'Aham' 'Aham' 'I'-'I'.

This is the sign that Pure Consciousness is beginning to reveal itself. But that is not the end in itself. Watch wherefrom this sphurana (throbbing) arises and wait attentively and continually for the revelation of the Self. Then comes the awareness, oneness of existence."

22.1.2001

Someone asked me the other day why I always pointed towards Sri Maharshi's teaching of Atma Vichara.

The reason is simplicity itself. To participate, it does not matter, where you live, whether male or female, young or old, what your culture is, what your status is, where you are, what you are doing. It does not need a set time or period of time to be effective. All that is needed is to pursue the question "Who am I?" Do your duty/work, but keep attention focussed on the enquiry. If pursued properly the enquiry leads to the Heart centre, the true 'I-I-I'.

2.2.2001

>*Is it possible for a person to renounce the EGO while leading the worldly life? It seems to be tricky one. Even if one says that I am leading a simple life with meagre needs, still there is an iota of EGO left behind. I am wondering whether it is possible to destroy the EGO while being in midst of worldly life.*<

Yes...assuredly!!

Perhaps these words from Ramana Maharshi will help.

"A jnani crushes the ego at its source. It rises up again and again, for him too as for the ignorant, impelled by nature i.e. prarabdha. Both in the ignorant and the jnani ego sprouts up but with this difference; the former's ego when it rises up is quite ignorant of its source, or is not aware of its deep sleep in the dream and wakeful states, whereas a jnani, when his ego rises up, enjoys his transcendental experience with his ego, keeping his lakshya [aim] always on its source. His ego is not dangerous, it is only the ash-skeleton of a burnt rope; although it possesses a form it is ineffective. By constantly keeping our lakshya on our source our ego is dissolved." (Talk 286)

19.2.2001 The need for remembrance

>*Imho, if there's no goal, there's no arriving there, and there's no failure... since arriving at a goal would be the same as getting nowhere, it seems much more purposeful to forget the need for goals entirely. There's nowhere to go and nothing to do – everything we need to know is inside us.*<

However... (at the risk of being untrendy): There is the goal: the experience of the non-dual Self. There is the means: Atma Vichara, Self Enquiry.

While we ARE the Self, for it alone is, ignorance causes us to imagine we have not realised it.

The following extract is taken from the introduction to 'Self Enquiry' [by Mahadevan]:

"The plenary experience of the non-dual Self is the goal; enquiry into the nature of the self is the means. When the mind identifies the self with the not-self (the body, etc.), there is bondage; when this wrong identification is removed through the enquiry 'Who am I ?' there is release. Thus, Self Enquiry is the direct path taught by Bhagavan Ramana. The 'I'-experience is common to all. Of all thoughts, the 'I'-thought is the first to arise. What one has to do is to enquire into the source of the 'I'-thought. This is the reverse process of what ordinarily happens in the life of the mind. The mind enquires into the constitution and source of everything else which, on examination, will be found to be its own projection; it does not reflect on itself and trace itself to its source. Self-discovery can be achieved by giving the mind an inward turn. This is not to be confused with the introspection of which the psychologists speak. Self Enquiry is not the mind's inspection of its own contents; it is tracing the mind's first mode, the 'I'-thought to its source which is the Self. When there is proper and persistent enquiry, the 'I'-thought also ceases and there is the wordless illumination of the form 'I'-'I' which is the pure consciousness. This is release, freedom from bondage. The method by which this is accomplished, as has been shown, is enquiry which, in Vedanta, is termed jnana, knowledge."

[http://nonduality.com/ramana3.htm]

Realisation is possible here... now... in this life. Of that, there is absolutely no doubt!!!Take up the Means!! Reach the Goal!!

19.2.2001 The need for remembrance

>*If you read more carefully you will see that the statement made by Joel Goldsmith refers to those who make NO effort. I.e. without effort you'll perhaps catch a glimpse of the Self but you'll not understand why it happened or how it happened or if it happened or if it'll happen again. namaste<*

True.

By constant practice of Atma Vichara the mind sinks readily, with true knowledge, in its source. The shepherd's search for the lamb believed lost, which is all the time lying over his shoulders and not lost, is still a search after all. Although close, without the search the lamb remains lost (see reference to 'shepherd' below).

From 'Self Enquiry' [in Collected Works, p. 32]:

"M: The jiva [individual soul] itself is Shiva; Shiva Himself is the jiva. It is true that the jiva is no other than Shiva. When the grain is hidden inside the husk, it is called paddy; when it is de-husked, it is called rice. Similarly, so long as one is bound by karma one remains a jiva; when the bond of ignorance is broken, one shines as Shiva, the Deity. Thus declares a scriptural text. Accordingly, the jiva which is mind is in reality the pure Self; but, forgetting this truth, it imagines itself to be an individual soul and gets bound in the shape of mind. So its search for the Self, which is itself, is like the search for the sheep by the shepherd. But still, the jiva which has forgotten its self will not become the Self through mere mediate knowledge. By the impediment caused by the residual impressions gathered in previous births, the jiva forgets again and again its identity with the Self, and gets deceived, identifying itself with the body, etc. Will a person become a high officer by merely looking at him? Is it not by steady effort in that direction that he could become a highly placed officer? Similarly, the jiva, which is in bondage through mental identification with the body, etc., should put forth effort in the form of reflection on the Self, in a gradual and sustained manner; and when thus the mind gets destroyed, the jiva would become the Self*.The reflection on the Self which is thus practised constantly will destroy the mind, and thereafter will destroy itself like the stick that is used to kindle the cinders burning a corpse. It is this state that is called release."

(* "Though the obstacles which cause the bondage of birth may be many, the root-cause for all such changes is ahankara [I-sense]. This root-cause must be destroyed for ever." – Vivekachudamani)

20.2.2001 Goal or not goal

>*Perhaps it's only semantics, as I think we both speak of the same realization. Is it a goal or is it not a goal? I don't know. Is it a paradox? May be.*<

"The 'I' casts off the illusion of 'I' and yet remains as 'I'. Such is the paradox of Self-Realisation. The realised do not see any contradiction in it." (from Talk 28)

>*I guess for me if I know I'm already there, that this life path is for returning to whence I came, then the goal has already been met. I'm already there. No need to have even this as a goal.*<

Indeed, there is nothing new to attain, only to be that which you always are and have always been. In essence the goal is simply to remove the veil-like covering of ignorance which obscures the Self. The ignorance being that of the ego-self which, assuming a stance separate from everything else, then looks at and acts on this falsely perceived as separate universe.

>*Perhaps this is why Ramana said the highest teaching is in silence. Beyond the need to define.*<

The jnani uses his own language, whether with or without words, it makes no difference.

23.2.2001

If we objectify this nothing (whatever it may be) we're lost. Instead find that which is the eternal, boundless and limitless subject, "...because there is nothing alien to the Self." (from Talk 42)

"Meditate on who you are. Quit imagining." To imagine what something (nothing) is... is to be lost. To search for 'it', as an objectified entity, will always be problematic. To search for the searcher however, to trace back to the sole source, is undoubtedly "...an easy thing." So easy in fact that it is regularly dismissed in a furious search for complications.

Analysis of the many is superseded by enquiry into the One. Nothing can be outside of this immediate, endless, unbroken, multi-dimensional Self.

It is 'my' subjective realisation which reveals this. Something exists only so long as there is some other to observe it. 'My' subjective realisation extends beyond this limited 'me'.

8.4.2001

>*I have trouble stopping the thoughts and doing Self Enquiry when I need to deal with people. And I need to deal with other people in many complex ways.*<

The practice of Atma Vichara should be continuous. No need to stop in the midst of daily life. If one forgets, simply take it up again when one remembers. Eventually the enquiry becomes a constant.

9.4.2001

>*I also still have not got a convincing reply to problems related to work. I would go to the extent of asking that, has somebody (let that somebody be of average credentials nay maybe inferior credentials though the same maybe partly due to circumstances) having full faith in Ramana got out of an unpleasant job (quitting without any standby options – normally everybody's advice is quit if you have an alternative on hand) and carving a niche for himself in life having confidence that his goodness and talent makes him deserve better without any prejudices towards his past employers. (i.e the ones he had left).*<

Yes!!

My life has been full of stops and starts. Some will-full others not. On more than one occasion I have "burnt my boat" (as my father used to say).The ONE constant is absolute faith in Bhagavan Sri Ramana and His Teaching. Whether or not I would advise such things to another is quite a different matter. How deep is your Faith?? The depth of your Faith is the only consideration in this. Who ... are ... you? Why do you need to get out? Is this simply ego too? Irrespective of the situation Atma Vichara is the key!!!!

>*Also I would like to state that this moment we are lucky that we can ask questions today and we have somebody to answer them. Tomorrow we may drift and get caught up in mundane activities forgetting Ramana's name and forums such as these to enhance one's spirituality and then remember only at the fag end of one's life. However as RAMANA has assured us it will definitely come alright at the 'End'. Let us pray that this 'End' comes sooner than later.*<

The 'end' comes right now... now... now... now (ad infinitum). The only barrier to this is the ego and its efforts to perpetuate itself. Act now. Atma Vichara is the means and the goal. Any delay is the not so subtle ploy of the ego.

3.5.2001 What is Self Enquiry?

>*I have read what Ramana Maharshi has said re: Self Enquiry, but I would like to know if you ask: "Who am I?" Should we really wonder? Or just listen after asking the question. Seems if I really wonder, I am digging and the pot is stirring rather than a flippant... "who am I" which doesn't stir anything... How do you inquire?*<

The enquiry searches for the source of the ego. The purpose is to focus the mind on its own source and rest there. The 'I'-thought is the root from whence all other thoughts arise. As long as any answer to the question is found, enquiry into the one (I) who finds answers is necessary. If one focusses in this way the mind (ego) vanishes and the Self remains self-evident.

"In the interior of the Heart-cave Brahman alone shines in the form of the Atman, self-evident, as 'I-I'." (Ramana Gita 2.2)

26.9.2001 Nothing but games

>*I see nothing but games!... Arbitrary, man-made games... Either one says: Well if it's all a hoax, the hell with all of it! ... Whether I die at the end of a healthy life or of liver trouble due to being an alcoholic or of AIDS... or of being chair-electrocuted due to a crime... or of yoga-standing on my head too long... or committing suicide, or of trying to open my third eye with a nail and hammer (as some tradition actually recommends)... it has no real meaning either way ...*

Or one closes the eyes to the what-is, and joins and sticks to the saving-raft/rope (or end of it) of one's choice... 'THE Way' or 'non- path', in great pink (& hidden) hopes... Or one consciously chooses to play the game of one's choice, worldly, social or spiritual, as if it was some 'absolute transcendental and ultimate reality or means thereto' or at least 'good enough for me'... Or one believes "it's all illusion" ... or "it's all God" ... Or one confesses "I know nothing!", while actually utterly drowning, in one of the above games. Or ... ?... one realises all this is entirely dependent on what the 'I', making the statement, is understood to be. Is he the ego or the Self?<

Consider the sun and the world actions... the sun is necessary for daily activities. He does not however form part of the world actions; yet they cannot take place without the sun. He is the witness of the activities. So it is with the Self. The ego acts in the presence of the Self. He cannot exist without the Self. So long as egoity lasts the games goes on. When egoity ceases to be, actions become spontaneous. The games might appear to go on but who on earth is playing them?

27.9.2001

>*Anyaway, I questioned, as that might be the one light, not belonging to this structure of endless models & paradigms (egoistic games)... or maybe not.<*

Inevitably the questions (and answers) are firmly encoded to the game. That does not mean they should not be asked but rather the reverse... they will be asked, irrespective of any denial pointed in that direction. It is always the ego who asks, it is always the ego who cannot find the answer. Even in denial, the question by default is hinted at. Look for it and it will not be found. That is the way.

5.2.2002 Is everything ordained?

>*I have to admit, this is the toughest part of Sri Bhagavan's teaching for me to understand. In fact, this is the only part that I have a difficult time with. While I can see his viewpoint in a situation like India in the past where there was little or no flexibility in terms of type of employment, culture, caste membership, and many other factors of life, I have seen too many here in the West, in modern times who seemed to have overcome the 'flow of fate' through concerted effort and prayerful action.*<

Things happen. Deeds are done. One can associate with the actions done with desire by this body/mind, and claim praise in success and deny blame in failure (or blame others etc.). Or one can turn to the Self in complete surrender. Everything happens according to prarabdha. This will exhaust itself if one surrenders to the Self. The path of desire gives the illusion of free-will to a fictitious individual ... the path of surrender submits to the will of the sole reality of the Self. This is jnana. This is bhakti. There is no I, no you etc., to claim free will or submit to predestination. There is nothing outside of the Self.

And from Conscious Immortality: "Whose freewill is it? You believe it is yours. You are beyond freewill and fate. Abide as that and you transcend them both." (Ramana Maharshi; see also Talk 209)

7.3.2002 How to develop humility?

>*There is a question for all here: During our sadhana at times we have to grapple with our egos –really king size :) How do you transcend your egoistic thoughts that erupt in your mind all the time? How do you develop humility?*<

Ego is an instrument of the Self. Other than this it has no independent existence. Sometimes it appears... sometimes not. Rather than carry the instrument around when it's not needed, remember to put it down. If through practice this remembrance becomes the default situation, there is no problem and no need to be concerned about developing (or not developing) humility.

29.3.2002

The simplest practice of all is Atma Vichara. That is Sri Ramana's gift to us. That is what is discussed here. Why give the mind fuel for thought when all that needs to be done is to "Seek the mind. On being sought, it will disappear. The mind is only a bundle of thoughts. The thoughts arise because there is a thinker. The thinker is the ego. The ego, if sought, will vanish automatically. The ego and the mind are the same. The ego is the root-thought from which all other thoughts arise. Dive within. You are now aware that the mind rises from within. So sink within and seek. You need not eliminate the wrong 'I'. How can 'I' eliminate itself? All that you need do is to find out its origin and abide there. Your efforts can extend only thus far. Then the beyond will take care of itself. You are helpless there. No effort can reach it." (from Conscious Immortality, p. 90)

"The intricate maze of philosophy of different schools is said to clarify matters and reveal the truth. But in fact, they create confusion where no confusion need exist. To understand anything there must be the Self. The Self is obvious. Why not remain as the Self?" (from Talk 392)

29.3.2002

> *"One early morning Sri Bhagavan explained how we have a glimpse of the real Self every day. 'Between sleep and waking there is a momentary twilight. The waking consciousness begins with the 'I' thought. Just before the upsurge of the 'I' thought, there is a split second of undifferentiated, pure consciousness. First unconsciousness, then the light of pure consciousness, then the 'I' thought with which the world-consciousness floods in, this is the order. The middle state is Self-awareness. We can sense it if we are sufficiently alert and watchful." (taken from G.V. Subbaramayya: Sri Ramana Reminiscences, p. 17)<*

Thank you for this sage piece of advice. This is a great place to start Atma Vichara. With practice Atma Vichara will start immediately on wake-up. What better way to start the day?!?!

30.3.2002

> *Unfortunately for me the dream state comes right after the deep sleep state and in the dream state there is for me a surreal sense of 'I'-consciousness and therefore I miss the pure consciousness state. So, to catch the transition from the deep sleep state to the dream state will take more mental power that I have right now. Anyone else have some thoughts on this?<*

In deep sleep one is in 'unconscious' Self-Realisation. There is no 'I' therefore only the Self exists. The Self exists throughout all three states. It is the only continuity, the true Identity. The individual has no continuity. If one can slow down the arising of 'ahamkara' [I-sense] in the transition from one state to another then one experiences That. The window of opportunity appears to be very small. What is required is vigilance.

Through Grace and the development of a continual process of Atma Vichara while awake, one automatically turns towards the Source at every opportunity. Then, just after sleep, at a time when ahamkara is weakest (just as it arises), Atma Vichara will automatically kick in. Gradually ahamkara can be held off for longer and longer periods. If this kind of discipline is practiced ahamkara gives way much more easily, and much more often. It is only thought that interferes.

1.4.2002

>*I am curious about the pronunciation of this... [om namo bhagavate sri ramanaya]. Could someone help me phonetically? Also is this just a greeting or can it be used as a mantra?*<

"Om namo bhagavate sri ramanaya" meaning: "I bow down, in humble obeisance (in surrender), to Lord Sri Ramana." What better mantra could there be for His devotee!?! It's a great 'cutter of thought' and prelude to Atma Vichara. It is the Supreme ajapa-japa.

Om
namo
bhagavatay (/ bh / is an aspirate / b / (slight aspiration)
shree
ramanaaya (/ n / is retroflex, the third syllable is long)

3.4.2002 Experiences

>*How is it possible to see the world and its objects as illusionary, as long one has to deal with it all?*<

Dealing with the world is part of the illusion. It is symptomatic of the human condition which, having forgotten its own Self, dwells in an external, material universe. As long as one does not see the Self as the origin of all, and one's very identity, so long can it (world and objects) be described as illusionary.

World and objects are creations of the mind. They exist in subjective consciousness. Jnana (knowledge of the Self) eliminates this false identity. This is effected by tracing the 'I' back to its source.

"Until there is the 'I'-thought, there will be no other thought. Until other thoughts arise, (asking) 'To whom?' (will call forth the reply) 'To me'. He who pursues this closely, questioning 'What is the origin of the 'I'?' and diving inwards reaches the seat of the mind (within) the Heart, becomes (there) the Sovereign Lord of the Universe. O boundless Ocean of Grace and Effulgence called Arunachala, dancing motionless within the court of the Heart! There is no (longer any) dream there of such dualities as in and out, right and wrong, birth and death, pleasure and pain, or light and darkness." (Eleven Verses to Arunachala, 7)

3.4.2002

>*When I sit for doing Vichara I start to watch my thoughts... but I get only a blank... but after sometime when I am engrossed in thoughts I am not able to watch my thoughts... I forget to watch the thoughts... This is my problem... Am I doing the correct way?... Please help me out.*<

If there is awareness of a blank then there is an observing subject. Perseverance with the practice of Atma Vichara will overcome it. Realising that you have been engrossed in thought is the Grace which provides impetus for continuing with Atma Vichara.

"One-pointed perseverance alone is essential in Self Enquiry and that is done purely inwardly, all the time. Your attention on the Self within alone is essential." (Moments Remembered, p. 77)

26.4.2002

>*I am asking you about how you are reacting to your "ill heath"? Has your practice and Ramana's teaching been of benefit to your experiencing of your body problems? Can you stay with the pain and return to your sense of conscious presence? Feel free not to respond to this inquiry.<*

We must, we should, each, examine these things for ourselves. What I have to say may be of no use. Here is a response to the inquiry.

There is never a return to consciousness. Rather consciousness is the unique, eternal, consistent 'experience'.

Pain is a natural response of the body. Who denies it? Like pleasure it can become a full on 'experience'. Where the problem might arise is in the denial, or non-acceptance, of the pain, resulting in the desire to replace it with something more pleasurable. Is pain separate from me? Is pleasure separate from me? Are pleasure and pain independent entities? By desiring pleasure and eschewing pain all is lost!! I take a painkiller and get a bit of relief.

Sometimes the body suffers and it is hard to stand up, sometimes a headache might interfere with daily tasks, with a broken leg it's no longer possible to long jump, etc. The body reacts accordingly. There's a process to go through. If that involves medical help, so be it.

Self Enquiry is a constant throughout all these 'experiences'/'processes'.

26.4.2002

>*As we have started to share our experiences and spiritual struggles here I come in with my struggle: it is fear of death, the fear of death of the ego, the fear to lose this identification with the body-mind, something which is very similar to what Major Chadwick reports in his reminiscences:*

"After I had been meditating in the presence of Bhagavan for some months, I reached a certain stage when I would be overcome by fear. I asked Bhagavan about this. I was assured by some of those present in the Hall at the time, not of course by Bhagavan, that this was all wrong and quite absurd. In fact they laughed at me for my foolishness. Bhagavan was not so amused. He explained that it was the ego that experienced the fear as it felt that it was gradually losing its grip. It was, in fact, dying, and naturally resented it. He asked me, 'To whom is the fear? It is all due to the habit of identifying the body with the Self. Repeated experience of separation from this idea will make one familiar with this state and fear will then automatically cease.'" (Sadhu Arunachala: A Sadhu's Reminiscences, p. 46f)

Sri Ramana once gave this beautiful reply to Chadwick and I take it also as a reply for me. I only wanted to share this, because there may be some here who have to deal with a similar struggle.<

A suggestion:

antakAle ca mAmeva smaranmuktvA kalevaram /
yah prayAti sa madbhAvam yAti nAstyatra saMSayah //
yaM yaM vApi smaranbhAvaM tyajatyante kalevaram /
taM tamevaiti kaunteya sadA tadbhAvabhAvitah //

"And the one, who, at the time of death, having abandoned the body, remembers Me alone, that one attains the True Nature of 'I'; in this there is no doubt. Whatever mental state one remembers, at the end, when one leaves the body, to that alone one goes, O Son of Kunti, (because of) ever 'thinking' of that state." (Bhagavad Gita, 8. 5,6)

This is the reason Self Enquiry, 'practice' is so important. At the time of death, the ego throws up all the reasons it can to show its (small) self-importance. It reflects on its life... desperate to sustain that life. It bemoans the loss of its family and friends. It screams that this cannot be happening to one so awfully important. It remembers its possessions. It dwells on property and business. All it is... is these random thoughts. All this seems like it takes an age... but happens in the blink of an eye. EGO PANICS. This is the time to catch it. If Self Enquiry has been rehearsed, in the 'strong' mind... it cuts in, finding ego weak and vulnerable, and eradicates all trace of ego... there and then. Of this there is absolutely no doubt. There is absolutely no doubt.

1.5.2002

>*I am still dealing with your reply. You speak here about the last moment before death. I experience now the same what you are describing. It also can happen in the process of Self Enquiry over a longer period of time. The ego does everything to come back to its normal strength and awareness and for this the body-mind goes on strike – everything is out of order – there is enormous suffering – everything outwardly becomes extremely difficult. Is this normal? Or is there something going wrong?*<

Self Enquiry is a continual practice. Whenever the mind forgets to enquire, which is its normal trait, it needs nudged back in the direction of enquiry. If this enquiry becomes the predominant habit of the mind... so be it.

As long as one identifies wrongly with the body so long will one see the world as an external manifestation, with consequent suffering. The solution is to seek the Reality first. At the time of death (at ego's weakest) the mind flails about in blind panic. During everyday life it seems self-assured of its existence. Even deep sleep is not feared, but rather welcomed, because the ego has experience of always reappearing. Its confidence is its weakness. At times this weakness becomes self-evident. When one wakes up for example. If Self Enquiry starts on wake up... or at times of observance of breath-taking beauty... etc. ego is caught unawares at these times. (shhh...don't tell it).

29.5.2002 Aham sphurana

>*In a certain context I came across that word 'aham shurana'. I remember that Ramana before his self-realization had sphurana of Arunachala. The meaning of 'sphurana' is not quite clear to me. I have only a vague idea that it has the meaning of 'pulsation' or 'vibration'. Can anyone here say more about? Where does this sphurana (pulsation of aham) happen? Is it in the spiritual Heart- centre? How is it experienced? What is its meaning in the context of Self Enquiry? What is it? Thanks in advance for every comment.<*

'Sphurana' can be translated in a variety of ways – flashing, glistening, quivering, vibrating, throbbing, coming into view, manifestation, etc.

In essence it is the primary manifestation of the Self in the body (the real source of creation). It is experienced when the flow of consciousness is reversed and thoughts/ego are traced back to the Heart centre (Hridaya). Some have experienced this as a physical manifestation on the right side of the chest. One may continue to sense a constant sphurana after revelation of the Self. In Absolute terms however there is no location. This is simply the centre without bounds.

16.6.2002

Vichara, when spontaneous, is not action. Meditation requires subject and object, whereas Vichara is, of necessity, devoid of object. Vichara is samadhi. Vichara is turiya. Samadhi is turiya. True Vichara is Realisation. Realisation is devoid of action.

samnyasya sarvakarmANi bhavabandhavimuktayeyatyatAm paNDitair dhIrair AtmAbhyAsa upasthitaih / 10 /

"Abandoning all actions in order to break free from the bond of birth and death, abidance in the Self is attained by the courageous wise man." (Vivekacudamani, 10)

20.6.2002 Truthfulness

>*Is truth in speech subjective and therefore varies according to ones conditioning?*<

Where truth is ... falsehood is not. Brahman is truth. The Self cannot be attained without practising truth. Suffering is the result of false relationships, false fears, false ideas. Liberation is truth. How is this liberation realised?

Through right action of mind, speech and body. That is jnana, that is freedom, that is moksha. Self Enquiry is constant truth. Maintaining the quest even in the midst of worldly duties ensures right action.

1.7.2002 Light

jyotishAmapi tajjyotistamasah paramucyate /
jnAnam jneyam jnAnagamyam hrdi sarvasya vishThitam //

"Light of lights, beyond the darkness, He is called; true knowledge, that which is to be investigated, understood through knowledge, abiding in the Heart of all." (Bhagavad Gita 13, 18)

That, which illumines all of this, is Light. Its nature is satya (Reality), the Self-luminous, Light of Consciousness (cidAbhAsa). As the sun illuminates the world, so the Light of lights (Atman) illuminates mind and senses. As the eye cannot see without the light of the sun, so the intellect cannot function without the Light of the Self.

It is said that the sun does not shine there, nor do the moon and the stars, nor lightning nor fire. All the lights in the universe cannot be compared even to a ray of this inner light of the Self. Conceptual twaddle falls away in obeisance to this Light of all. Take to Vichara and merge yourself in this constant, eternal light of lights, the light of the Self.

Blazing, Sri Arunachala, a seemingly insentient hill, silently representing Siva/Paramatman, reveals the mystery of the Self to one who enters through the fire of Vichara.

7.7.2002

>*I also agree with you perception of the two-step process. Inquiry starts with the mind, then moves past it.*<

While this may be argued from the theoretical standpoint, in order to draw attention to misplaced identity, it has no substance in reality. Even to say that Self Enquiry has one step is to miss the point. When the Self is sought, the mind is nowhere. Atma Vichara is process and goal. Absolutely nothing happens without the Self. Realisation is to get rid of the delusion that you have not realised. The Self is always realised. This is not dependent on any theoretical school of thought, whether advaita or dvaita, nor with any practice. It is simply the true state of affairs.

8.7.2002

>*In principle you are correct but this is generally not how practice progresses.*<

Thank you.

The point made is simply that while practice is all important, if one clings to any intellectual idea of 'progress' or steps within the process, there is self-entrapment in the net of degrees of growth etc. There is absolutely no linear progression. The idea of steps is only in the mind. This is the experience here. All practice is simply a rehearsal for the spontaneous, absolute enquiry which is our nature. In spontaneous enquiry there is neither step, progression nor movement. There is only the Self. Practice Vichara, until it becomes automatic throughout life, but leave open the door to spontaneity (effortlessness). This is Grace.

9.7.2002

>*Certainly my teacher, who teaches 'no-creation' (so therefore there is nothing to attain and no one to attain it), teaches of the need for practice.*<

Indeed. Practice is essential (abhyasa vairagyabhyam – by practice and non-attachment). The mind must grow 'strong', practice is the means. Through continued strength of practice the mind begins to fly to Vichara at every opportunity. This is what is meant by 'automatic'. Like a man with his head held under water longs for air so the mind as soon as distracted by the lures of the world must immediately seek Vichara. With practice that which once, apparently, took intense effort becomes effortlessness.

>*He also teaches that practice mainly consists of eliminating the erroneous ideas (super-impositions) that show up as identification with the world or body or senses or prajna or mind. When all these are removed, then the seeker will be able to identify as, to stand as, Being-Conscious-Bliss.*<

Neti neti – not this, not this – while useful, this tends to be an intellectual practice. On this Sri Ramana has said:

"D.: I begin to ask myself 'Who am I?', eliminate the body as not 'I', the breath as not 'I', the mind as not 'I' and I am not able to proceed further.

M.: Well, that is so far as the intellect goes. Your process is only intellectual. Indeed, all the scriptures mention the process only to guide the seeker to know the Truth. The Truth cannot be directly pointed out. Hence this intellectual process.

You see the one who eliminates all the 'not I' cannot eliminate the 'I'. To say 'I am not this' or 'I am that' there must be the 'I'. This 'I' is only the ego or the 'I'-thought... Therefore seek the root, question yourself 'Who am I?'; find out its source." (Talk 197)

>*In my own experience, not until I choose to practice regularly did much deep progress occur.<*

It must go beyond choice. It must become a necessity.

>*I have also heard Nome warn against negating the need to practice by use of nonduality as an idea rather than as where one actually stands.<*

Indeed. The idea 'non-duality' is only valid as opposition to 'duality'... neither has anything to do with the Quest, Being.

9.7.2002

>*In terms of Ramana's recommendations on negation (neti, neti), I repost from 'Who am I', paragraph 3:*

"Therefore, summarily rejecting all the above-mentioned physical adjuncts and their functions, saying 'I am not this; no, nor am I this, nor this' – that which remains separate and alone by itself, that pure Awareness is what I am. This Awareness is by its very nature Sat-Chit-Ananda (Existence-Consciousness-Bliss)."

This seems to fit with what my teacher says about the importance of eliminating the illusion to clear the field for the Real.<

Indeed, I don't see any disagreement here, the point being that the understanding that comes from 'neti neti' remains mindstuff without the quest 'Who am I?'As a preliminary understanding it is indeed helpful. In the ultimate analysis however to say 'I am this' or 'I am not that' remains in the realm of limitations.

In Sri David Godman's 'Be As You Are', chapter 6 gives numerous examples of this very important point. Later in the text you have quoted there appears the statement "Since every other thought can occur only after the rise of the 'I'-thought and since the mind is nothing but a bundle of thoughts, it is only through the enquiry 'Who am I?' that the mind subsides." (from 'Who am I?') Even the affirmation 'I am Brahman' or the negation 'I am not this body' leaves the 'I' who makes the declaration... Who is it? Ultimately, once again, we are lead to investigation of the Self. This is the point.

10.7.2002

>*But what Miles was stating is that practice isn't necessary and that inquiry should be spontaneous or random which is something different.*<

Enquiry is deliberate... never random. Practice is all important. Spontaneity (unforced, natural) is manifestation of ever flowing Grace when strength of mind ensues. Then that which has taken effort becomes effortless.

17.7.2002

>*I validate this Ramana Guru Bhakti faction.*<

They are all valid (bhakti, jnana, karma). While the teachings of the sages are suited to time, place and other considerations, in the end, all leads to the place where, having abandoned lokavichara, one submits to Atma Vichara.

18.7.2002

>*What is lokavichara? I am not sure I understand your point right.*<

Lokavichara is paying attention to the world of externals rather than holding the substratum of the 'I'. Whereas Atma Vichara opens the 'secret' of the Self and reveals that the world is unreal apart from the underlying Reality.

7.8.2002

In the second chapter of Sri Ramana Gita, Sri Bhagavan gives, in four lines of Sanskrit, the essence of His teaching.

Hrdayakuharamadhye kevalam brahmamAtram hyahama-
hamiti sAkshAdAtmarupeNa bhAti |
hrdi viSa manasA svam cinvatA majjatA vA
pavanacalanarodhAdAtmanishTho bhava tvam ||
(Ramana Gita 2. 2)

In the inmost core, the Heart
Shines as Brahman alone,
As 'I-I', the Self aware.
Enter deep into the Heart
By searching for Self, or diving deep,
Or with breath under check.
Thus abide ever in Atman.

This verse reveals the Self and three methods for the Realisation of the Self which encompass jnana, bhakti and Yoga.

Hrdayakuharamadhye kevalam brahmamAtram

In the interior cave of the Heart, Brahman alone shines, no more – no less. This Heart is the seat of the Self. This Heart is none other than Brahman. You are always in the Heart. You are, indeed, this Heart. This is the Self. In truth the Self is without location... but in order to help the sadhak and to give direction, in His compassion, Sri Bhagavan has pointed us towards the middle of our being.

"The Heart is not physical; it is spiritual. Hridayam = hrit + ayam = This is the centre. It is that from which thoughts arise, on which they subsist and where they are resolved. The thoughts are the content of the mind and they shape the universe. The Heart is the centre of all. Yatova imanibhutani jayante (that from which these beings come into existence) etc. is said to be Brahman in the Upanishads. That is the Heart. Brahman is the Heart." (from Talk 97)

We should not allow ourselves to be drawn by distinctions of physical and spiritual. The physical is entirely dependent on the spiritual. The spiritual is never dependent on the physical (i.e. the distinction is simply false perception). Although referred to as Heart centre, this is entirely without centre or circumference; everything, body and all else, exists within it.

"This space within the Heart is as vast as the (physical) space outside. Indeed, within it are both heaven and earth; fire and air; sun and moon; lightning and stars. Whatever is in this world and whatever is not... all that is established within it." (Chandogya Upanishad, 8.1.3)

hyahamahamiti sAkshAdAtmarupeNa bhAti |

As 'I', as 'I', the Self aware; Self-evidently shining. Continuous and uninterrupted.

"D.: What is the Heart?

M.: It is the seat (if such could be said of it) of the Self.

D.: Is it the physical Heart?

M.: No. It is the seat wherefrom 'I'–'I' arises." (from Talk 52)

Can we recognise/experience the Self in the body? Yes we can. Atma Vichara is the key. Once unlocked the 'I'–'I' consciousness shines forth directly, unobstructed.

hrdi viSa manasA svam cinvatA majjatA vA
pavanacalanarodhAdAtmanishTho bhava tvam ||

How do we submerge the mind in the Heart? Three methods are suggested. Quest for Self. This is jnana. Diving deep. This is bhakti. Attraction of/to the Self with or without attributes. Breath control. This is the path of Yoga. In essence all three are resolved in one (Atma Vichara). "Thus abide ever in Atman."

11.9.2002 Yoga - the Heart of all things

>*If anybody can find a quotation in which Bhagavan tells people to deliberately focus attention on the right side of the chest as a technique, I would be fascinated to see it. I don't think I've ever seen one.*<

In 'Self Enquiry' Bhagavan states, "The loci that are eminently fit for meditation are the Heart and Brahma-randhra (aperture in the crown of the head). One should think that in the middle of the eight-petalled lotus that is at this place there shines like a flame, the Deity which is the Self, i.e. Brahman, and fix the mind therein. After this, one should meditate." (Collected Works, p. 22f)

Elsewhere, in this text, the location and various revelations on Heart are also given.

12.9.2002 Self Enquiry and the Heart

>*In this teaching I have not seen any emphasis on the 'Heart.' Inquiry is describes as 'formless.'*<

Formless/formfull who cares? These dichotomies will resolve themselves.

Sri Ramana has said: "The source of the 'I' is the Heart – the final goal." The easiest and most direct, "the first and foremost step to be taken", is enquiry. If one is not suited to Vichara, other means, such as meditation on a 'centre' or 'neti neti' or pranayama etc., are adopted initially. The Heart is the Self. That is the source of the mind. All else is mere polemics.

>*I spent several years using the right-hand-side-of-the chest 'Heart centre' as a focus in my inquiry. Certainly the sensation from this centre is the most constant 'sensation' that comes from this body.*<

The irresistible pull of the Heart is not a sensation of mind. It is the supreme continuity. While it can appear physical it is not reliant on the physical. It is not objective. It becomes apparent when the contents of the mind dissipate, when ego begins to lose hold. It is the original expression of Self. If one can take to Self Enquiry this is the inevitable result.

Sri Ramana once said that He "... could feel the action of the physical heart stopped and equally the action of the Heart centre unimpaired. This state lasted about a quarter of an hour." Apparently "... some disciples have had the privilege of feeling Sri Bhagavan's Heart centre to be on the right by placing their hands on Sri Bhagavan's chest." (from Talk 403)

>*When I ask questions to Nome about my practice, he has been generally encouraging – as long as it gets to "Who am I?" Indeed. This is the crux. I write this as a seeker, though, not as one who stands in Self-Realization, so much of my knowledge is 'indirect' (that is, through indirect means such as the mind). Ramana taught from 'direct' knowledge. Nome teaches from 'direct' knowledge.<*

Direct/indirect – it makes no odds. Claims to directness or indirectness just exacerbate the problem for the seeker. All that is necessary is to take to Atma Vichara ...

12.9.2002

>*1. Trace the I-thought to its source. 2. All thoughts vanish. 3. A throb arises from the Heart centre. 4. Watch that place.<*

Indeed. This is exactly what happens.

12.9.2002

>*If a person tries to focus on the Heart centre before it announces itself with the sphurana, then they may imagine a*

Heart centre. Instead of falling into the real one, they may imagine something. Then they focus on that imaginary something. It remains an object and their sense of subjecthood remains intact. In other words, they end up doing the kind of meditation that's common in Tantric Yoga and Tai Chi.<

This is not a problem. One might surmise that this instruction was indeed given to Arthur Osborne and he in turn relates it to whoever is interested. The focus is designed to eliminate extraneous thought. The Enquiry then catches the one who focusses. Not all sadhakas are necessarily given the same practice. Different folk different capacities. But... it is all Vichara in the end.

21.9.2002

>Here for reaching the Heart breath control is also suggested as a means. Perhaps someone can say something about who has practiced.<

>I would appreciate it if any one has any practical advice on this practice. The Ashram published a book called 'The Technique of Maha Yoga'. It suggested focussing on the Heart centre on an exhalation after breath retention. I prefer focussing and diving on the retention. What do others find best for them?<

When talking about samadhi, Sri Bhagavan spoke of "...the stillness of a waveless ocean..." (from Talk 406) What a wonderful expression! When the breath comes under control, this 'stillness' is experienced. Control can be forced, as in various 'hatha yoga' practices, or spontaneous as mentioned in Sri Ramana Gita, chapter 6:

prANarodhaSca manasA prANasya pratyavekSaNam /
kumbhakam sidhyati hyevam satatapratyavekSaNAt //

Control of the breath is attention to the flow of breath by the mind. In this way, through constant attention, kumbhaka [retention of breath] is accomplished.

Mind and breath spring from the same source so controlling one automatically controls the other. However, in practice, constantly watching the breath seems to be easier, and more efficacious, than forcibly controlling it. I seem to remember Sri Bhagavan compared the two methods to the milking of a cow. The first to cajoling the cow by feeding her grass and gently patting her back and the latter to forcibly milking her, whether she likes it or not. Those who have used both methods have reported that there may be a danger of falling into laya (unconsciousness) when using forcible control, therefore nullifying any subsequent Enquiry. Whereas simple attention (pratyavekSaNa) when coupled with Atma Vichara results in kumbhaka and the sphurana arising spontaneously from the Heart (with or without physical manifestation). It seems the gentle cajoling method is Sri Bhagavan's first recommendation and hatha yoga methods are recommended for those who are unable to achieve kumbhaka (which is nothing more or less than sahajasthiti – abidance in the Self) this way. It certainly is the method used here.

11.11.2002

This passage was posted some time back on Ramana Maharshi list, in a conversation we had. Perhaps it helps the search for a quotation in which Sri Bhagavan ... "tells people to deliberately focus attention on the right side of the chest as a technique".

"In the course of tracing ourselves back to our source, when all thoughts have vanished, there arises a throb from the Hridaya on the right, manifesting as 'Aham' 'Aham' 'I'- 'I'. This is the sign that Pure Consciousness is beginning to reveal itself. But that is not the end in itself. Watch wherefrom this sphurana (throbbing) arises and wait attentively and continually for the revelation of the Self. Then comes the awareness, oneness of existence." (from a reply, approved by Bhagavan, which was sent to an English devotee; recorded in 'Moments Remembered' by V. Ganesan, p. 53)

This is a clear statement... or is it? In any case, it is the experience of some who practice Atma Vichara that their resistible pull to a specific point, namely the Hridaya on the right side, results in a 'deliberate' watching, followed by a spontaneous revelation. Even after such episode the throbbing can (but does not always) continue for a time. As far as this being a technique... who knows? It certainly 'could' be taken for one.

Earlier in this same statement it is stated... "If by meditation or Vichara we attain to our centre, the Hridaya, and thus are our real Self, we enjoy unalloyed bliss."

Hridaya is described in various ways in this piece... i.e. 'the seat of God in us', 'the seat of Pure Consciousness', 'different from the physical heart', 'has its being on the right side and is not commonly known or felt', 'the literal, actual, physical seat of the intuition of the Self.' It goes on to say '... the word 'physical seat' may create some confusion of thought. What it really means is that there is a centre of Pure Consciousness in the physical body. It is related to the physical but is not itself physical. This is experiential. Perhaps one should just take to Atma Vichara and find out for oneself. Whether one starts with attention focussed on the Hridaya is immaterial. It is certainly not a necessity for Vichara. However, it has been said that it is an inevitable conclusion.

28.11.2002

>A strange thing is that when Vichara becomes an earnest practice the mind starts to trouble enormously. This is so here with me. The mind is sometimes so much agitated, that one really wonders how this practice should be done. Mind-

stuff is coming up enormously. But what I remember is, that Bhagavan has said, that this is normal. Vasanas come to surface. So that's ok.

Sadhu Om somewhere said that this is the grace of the Guru. Vichara seems to be a very powerful cleansing process, something like the purgatory in Christianity, not pleasant for the ego. Somewhere I have read that Vichara is bliss from beginning to the end. I can't agree. It is a hard graft, that's for sure. Peace will then set in more and more, but purification has to happen first.<

I'm maybe pretty stupid but it seems that there is an inordinate desire to create something complicated out of something which is inherently extremely simple. The problem is mindstuff (thought chasing thought, becoming tied up in more thought and adding to the bundle of thoughts already thought, all being dragged around in a little car behind oneself, or before oneself) and the solution is halting it.

To halt mindstuff Self Enquiry is employed. Self Enquiry is simply becoming aware of aberrant thought and asking to whom it appears. This is it. All the rest is more mindstuff. The increased activity in the mind is a misnomer. All that happens is awareness of the absurdity of thought becomes heightened. If one practices, Self Enquiry cuts in more and more often, feelings of peace increase (i.e. there is the realisation that mind doesn't need to pander to incessant thought, thought becomes a clutter) and eventually it goes on all day, all night. Until... something happens... ego comes up against its worst fear... annihilation. For me it was a bang on the head followed by a continual beating and a quick rush in the ambulance, during which there was resuscitation, followed by a few days in hospital.

11.3.2003 Quiet is boring?

Boredom? :)

Boredom is mindstuff! The one who is bored is the very problem. Without him how could there possibly be boredom? This is the human condition. Comparisons between this and that, between activity and boredom. There is absolutely no boredom in awareness. You decide that there must be something more interesting to do and declare yourself bored. This is not awareness. This is mindstuff. Simple pandering to the monkey-mind. If one attends to Self Enquiry throughout daily life, rather than just at times of seated meditation, this is very easily overcome, without loss of 'entertainment'. Self Enquiry is vibrant, never boring. It efficiently eliminates the one who is bored!

29.5.2003

>*When I try to find the source of the 'I' thought, I find that in my case it seems to be located in the head and not on the right side of the Heart. And if I try to locate the 'I' in the Heart, I find that the 'I' in the head is trying to monitor the progress of the one in the Heart to see if he is securely resting there. Now there cannot be two 'I's. If I try to investigate, I find that the 'I' in the head is the witness of the one in the Heart. That does not seem alright because it is contrary to Ramana's teaching. Has anyone faced a similar problem or can anyone with more experience in Self Enquiry offer me some help? Many thanks and regards.*<

This is indeed an interesting question and one that sadhakas often shy away from asking. Perhaps because the answer can be construed as the proverbial slap in the face.

Often investigation is made in the mind and remains firmly rooted by the 'I'-thought itself. Ahamkara [the I-sense] survives through objective association. Looking for a location stimulates this. If you perceive 'I' anywhere then there is subject-object association. The Self is not dependent on location. There should be nothing associated with the Self. Instead, investigate what the mind is and it will disappear.

Other than thought there is absolutely nothing that can be called mind. Mind is dependent on the arising of the primary thought 'I', alone. This 'I'-thought must be uprooted. Your 'I' in the head and 'I' in the heart are both symptomatic of the primary 'I'-thought. If this was not the case then the above question would not occur. It is common to intellectualize the process of Vichara without realising it. Instead one must be open to Grace. Ask the question... don't look for an answer. Consider the physical terms head and heart to be arbitrary, they have nothing to do with Vichara and everything to do with polemics. Vichara attracts polemical discourse. This is, of course, mindstuff.

The quest is of sole importance. Any answer that comes to mind when the question 'Who am I?' is asked... must be enquired into. All thoughts must vanish... "In the course of tracing ourselves back to our source, when all thoughts have vanished, there arises a throb from the Hridaya on the right, manifesting as 'Aham' 'Aham' 'I'-'I'. This is the sign that Pure Consciousness is beginning to reveal itself. But that is not the end in itself. Watch wherefrom this sphurana (throbbing) arises and wait attentively and continually for the revelation of the Self. Then comes the awareness, oneness of existence." (Moments Remembered, p. 53)

When aham sphurana arises from the still depths of the Heart, when this spontaneously happens, there may indeed be a sensation on the right side of the chest. However the location head/heart is not important for Vichara. Aham sphurana is the trumpet call of the Self.

With practice, Vichara becomes the default situation throughout the day and night. It goes on during conversation, at work, in times of abstract silence. Then success is assured.

31.1.2003

>*There is some risk, though, for a seeker without a teacher.*

The risk is that the seeker's own ego may direct (and limit) the practice. Also, as you say, there is risk from the 'sharks swimming in the ocean.'<

Perhaps one needs to understand and trust that everything unfolds exactly as it should. That the sharks swimming in this ocean are in fact akin to tiddlers, both share the ocean and rely on it for their sustenance. Ego only appears to direct the practice. When the practice matures there never was an ego. This is part of the mystery, part of the quest. One can end up in deep, dangerous water with or without a teacher. It really doesn't matter. Best idea is to make a sincere effort to learn to swim (or rather dive) oneself. Then if the teacher's swimming is just theoretical there's no problem. And if another teacher is needed that teacher will be there. But this desire for association, this separation, the human condition, is the problem. If one clears the mind then there can be no false sage. If one truly loves the Sage as our very Self everything spontaneously falls into place.

2.2.2003

>I practiced Vichara continually. While walking or even while talking. This had also been my habit with mantra. I would keep my mantra constantly every moment of the day.<

This is wonderful. Vichara may be done even when engaged in work, indeed at all times. As Sri Bhagavan said: "Now what is your real nature? Is it writing, walking, or being? The one unalterable reality is Being. Until you realise that state of pure being you should pursue the enquiry. If once you are established in it there will be no further worry." (from Talk 596) Didn't Sri Bhagavan declare: "Vichara is the process and the goal also. 'I AM' is the goal and the final Reality. To hold to it with effort is Vichara. When spontaneous and natural it is Realisation." [from Talk 390] It seems that often the practice is limited only to allotted times, what a shame!

14.2.2003

>*Is not Vichara bhakti to the Self, surrender to the source? Can it be seen like this?*<

Indeed. Complete self-surrender is not different from Atma Vichara. The bhakta wanders through this world thinking only of Him. The anguish which arises if he were to forget for even a second is such that he immediately re-directs his attention to the Source of his affection. The true bhakta lives in a world of pure love where selfishness (or ego) is no more than a wispy cloud which is easily evaporated by the sun (of Devotion).

18.4.2003

The human condition occurs when one individuates and sees oneself as separate from Brahman (the Self). Man's struggle for release is thwarted so long as he claims birth, death, and reincarnation, within the limits of waking, dream and dreamless sleep as his own. 'I am', the blissful Self, is the natural experience which transcends ego, mind, intellect and senses. I exist as the Self of the universe, the universe exists in Me. "I am the Self, dwelling in the Heart of all beings, I am the beginning, the middle and also the end of all beings." (Bhagavad Gita 10, 20)

"To enquire 'Who am I?' really means trying to find out the source of the ego or the 'I'-thought. You are not to think of other thoughts, such as 'I am not this body, etc.' Seeking the source of 'I' serves as a means of getting rid of all other thoughts. We should not give scope to other thoughts,... (such as 'I am not this mortal body' or 'Why has God created this world?'],... but must keep the attention fixed on finding out the source of the 'I' thought, by asking (as each thought arises) to whom the thought arises and if the answer is 'I get the thought' by asking further who is this 'I' and whence its source?" (from 'Who am I?')

30.9.2003 Self can be experienced

The Self is the primal experience. This is the only real experience. All else is modification, imagining, built on a false premise.

"There is no one who even for a trice fails to experience the Self." (from Talk 97)

30.9.2003 Self can be experienced

>*I am sure 'experience' is NOT the word Sri Ramana used. Simply because, 'experience' as generally understood implies the existence of the trio – experiencer-experienced-experiencing.<*

Why should the word 'experience' be problematic? It occurs throughout advaitic literature. If it is problematic, it is only because of the inadequacy of language and our semantic preconceptions. Below are a couple of examples which immediately spring up. 'Ordinary' experience is viparIta (different from real).

"The thought 'I', 'mine' erroneously imposed on the body and senses, which are not the real self, must be removed by the wise, by abiding as the real Self." (Vivekacudamani)

Experience implies 'trayi vidya' (the triad) only after the arising of ahamkara ('I', 'mine' etc.). The Self experiences itself eternally. However the mind trying to experience the Self is like the image in a mirror declaring its self-existence and that it is the one experiencing the origin of the image. The mind's experience is of the triad... and this is falsehood.

"The duality of subject and object and the trinity of seer, sight, and seen can exist only if supported by the One. If one turns inward in search of that One Reality they fall away. Those who see this are those who see Wisdom. They are never in doubt." (from Forty Verses, 9)

"An illness is not cured just by saying the name of the medicine without drinking it, and you will not be liberated by merely saying the word 'God', without direct experience (parokSAnubhavam)." (Vivekacudamani, 62) The direct experience reconciles the experiencer, the experienced and the experiencing.

"That we experience (anubhUyate) the bliss of the Self free from the senses in deep sleep is verified by the scriptures, by direct [self-evident] experience (pratyaksham), by tradition and by deduction." (Vivekacudamani, 107)

The word 'sAkshAt' is used by Sri Maharshi in Ramana Gita, 2.2. This refers to direct and Self-evident experience which is not reliant on anything other than itself.

In the inmost core, the Heart
Shines as Brahman alone,
As 'I'-'I', the Self aware
Enter deep into the Heart
By search for Self, or diving deep,
Or with breath under check.
Thus abide ever in Brahman.

>*One should not translate 'literally' what the great one says.*<

There is nothing cryptic about the Maharshi's words. That is their beauty. Attempting to interpret in terms of the triad is the only mistake.

From Talk 78; "Everyone has experience of the Self every moment of his life."

Instead of analysing and discussing this we should investigate this mindstuff, find its source, elimination of this non-self reveals the Self which being always self-evident will shine forth of itself.

1.11.2003 Kevala kumbhaka (retention of breath)

>*In Self Enquiry, it is mentioned that 'kevala kumbhaka' is/can be an aide to inquiry – sounded as if it were a breath-exercise. Does anyone know how to do this? Thanks<*

In Talks 448 Bhagavan gives a description of kumbhaka, as it pertains to Vichara.

"Naham – I am not this – corresponds to rechaka
Koham – Who am I? (search for the I) – corresponds to puraka
Soham – He am I; (The Self alone) — corresponds to kumbhaka.

So these are the functions of pranayama [breath-control].

Again the three formulae are:Na - Aham (Not - I).
Ka - Aham (Who - I).
Sa - Aham (He - I)

Delete the prefixes and hold on to the common factor in all of them. That is Aham – 'I', that is the gist of the whole matter."

For the jnani, kevala kumbhaka (retention alone) is quite simply spontaneous abidance in the Self. This retention is the natural conclusion of discrimination and enquiry. On the face of it, the jnani appears to breath like anyone else, however his mental stillness indicates kevala kumbhaka, as antah pranayama (internal breath control) as opposed to bahih pranayama (external breath control). The latter is mentioned here and there in the literature, in chapter 6, Mind-control, of Sri Ramana Gita for example. However even here where hatha yoga breathing ratios are mentioned, it is pointed out that jnanis define rechaka as giving up the 'I-am-the-body' idea, puraka is the quest for the Self and kumbhaka is abidance in the Self or sahaja sthiti. Antah pranayama is undoubtedly the preferred method for those who can take to it. If not then simply watching the breath will suffice to bring about spontaneous kumbhaka. Or constant association with enlightened Sages. Or repetition of mantras. Finally, if none of the above are possible, then hatha yoga breathing might be tried under supervision.

24.1.2004 Your own actual experience

>*I would like to read anyone's own actual experience/feelings/etc. which follows the question: "What is the origin of the I?" What happens to you? Where do you go? What's it like? How does it feel/look/sound/taste/etc. in your own personal words like "I feel/felt..."? Please state the exact sequence of events/feelings/thoughts, etc. that you, personally, experience/encounter after the question about your/the I.*<

28.1.2004 Re: Your own actual experience

>*I would like to read anyone's own actual experience/feelings/etc. which follows the question: "What is the origin of the I?"*<

Is this a philosophical enquiry or is it an enquiry into actual practice? If the latter then I would respond that during the practice of enquiry any answer/experience/feeling/etc. has validity only as a conduit to further enquiry into the 'I'. Whether the ego screams and thrashes in the throes of its annihilation or basks in its perception of the 'bliss of the Self' the enquiry must continue. Whether I declare (to myself) my identity in relation to family, friends, home, love of life, health etc. or profess a knowing oneness enquiry must continue. Whether fear or joy at this time go off the scale, the experiencer must be enquired into. As long as 'I' experience, this is the time for intense Self Enquiry. When quest for 'I' is finally discovered to be as valid as the mythical haggis hunt – who is left to discuss the 'actual experience/feelings/etc.'?

>*What happens to you?*<

You follow the same fate as me and he etc. When the sense of 'I' arises so too do the other persons, when the sense of 'I' is extinguished the other persons are also lost.

>*Where do you go?*<

I, he, you etc. are resolved as Self alone. If this is not the case then the enquiry remains ongoing.

>*What's it like?*<

It's like cooking skirlie.

>*How does it feel/look/sound/taste/etc.?*<

As the feel/look/sound/taste/etc. of successful skirlie cooking is skirlie-like alone so the feel/look/sound/taste/etc. of 'it' is to itself.

>*In your own personal words like "I feel/felt..." please state the exact sequence of events/feelings/thoughts, etc. that you, personally, experience/encounter after the question about your/the I.*<

In proper Enquiry there is no sequence of thought other than the reiteration of the enquiry, for as soon as any thought/feeling etc. arises 'I' ask 'myself' the question "To whom does this thought (feeling etc.) arise?" and scythe it down. What the thoughts, feelings etc. are is unimportant... What is important is the continuous remembrance of the enquiry into 'my' thoughts.

4.2.2004 Awareness watching awareness

>*Hi, I joined this group because I believe the best way to progress in the practice of Atma Vichara is by sharing our ideas and experiences on the subject. Well I think the members of this group are perhaps aware that even when Lord Ramana was alive the practice was not clearly understood by even those living in the ashram. So there are many differ-*

ent views on what the practice is. I don't wish to start a debate on the subject but I'd like the members of this group to help me out.

First of all there are some who say Atma Vichara is "awareness watching awareness" but others who claim that one's attention should be fixed on the one who is watching. According to Humphrey's who was very close to Ramana was personally advised by Lord Ramana to fix one's attention on the one who is watching. Those were Humphrey's exact words.

I'd like the members of this sangham to tell me from their own experience which is the more effective technique. I think those who practice the Vichara need to share their ideas and experiences on a regular basis. Further I'd like to know what Sadhu Om, a realised devotee of Lord Ramana, meant by self attention in his book 'The path of Ramana'. I've been practicing the Vichara for over 4 years. The Vichara has helped me in dealing with my day to day problems and trials quite competently but my spiritual life needs a boost for me to be really happy. So help me improve my technique in doing the Vichara. You may even write to me personally. I'd love to hear your personal opinions of what you think the Vichara is!<

>I'd like the members of this sangham to tell me from their own experience which is the more effective technique.<

The following is, for me, the most effective technique of Vichara. It became a constant companion.

From 'Who am I?':

"10. How will the mind become quiescent?

By the inquiry 'Who am I?' The thought 'who am I?' will destroy all other thoughts, and like the stick used for stirring the burning pyre, it will itself in the end get destroyed. Then, there will arise Self-realization.

11. What is the means for constantly holding on to the thought 'Who am I?'

When other thoughts arise, one should not pursue them, but should inquire: 'To whom do they arise?' It does not matter how many thoughts arise. As each thought arises, one should inquire with diligence, 'To whom has this thought arisen?' The answer that would emerge would be 'To me'. Thereupon if one inquires 'Who am I?', the mind will go back to its source; and the thought that arose will become quiescent. With repeated practice in this manner, the mind will develop the skill to stay in its source. When the mind that is subtle goes out through the brain and the sense-organs, the gross names and forms appear; when it stays in the Heart, the names and forms disappear. Not letting the mind go out, but retaining it in the Heart is what is called 'inwardness' (antarmukha). Letting the mind go out of the Heart is known as 'externalisation' (bahir-mukha). Thus, when the mind stays in the Heart, the 'I' which is the source of all thoughts will go, and the Self which ever exists will shine. Whatever one does, one should do without the egoity 'I'. If one acts in that way, all will appear as of the nature of Siva (God)."

Here are some useful hints shared by devotees who lived with Bhagavan:

In 'Moments Remembered' Sri Sadhu Natananda, author of 'Spiritual Instruction' and longtime resident in the vicinity of the Ashram, relates (p. 5): "On one occasion, I asked Bhagavan the right method for Atma Vichara and He replied: (i) "At any time and under all circumstances one should unfailingly remember one's real nature (I AM). (ii) While remembering this as one fulfils one's obligations in the world, one will do it without the least attachment to actions done, or to their results. When this attitude is strengthened the aspirant feels assured that he is making progress in his sadhana. (iii) This attitude should be practised by all."

Again from 'Moments Remembered' (p. 77), Sri M.G. Shanmugam relates: "He (Bhagavan) once said categorically: 'For practising Atma Vichara every day is auspicious and every moment is good, no discipline is prescribed at all. Any time, anywhere it can be done, even without others noticing that you are doing it. All other sadhanas require external objects and congenial environment, but for Atma Vichara nothing external to oneself is required. Turning the mind within is all that is necessary. While one is engaged in Atma Vichara one can with ease attend to other activities also. ... With attention focussed on the first person and on the Heart within, one should relentlessly practise Who am I? When this is done one-pointedly, one's breathing will subside of itself. During such controlled practice, the mind might suddenly spring up; so you have to vigilantly pursue the Vichara, Who am I?'"

>*First of all there are some who say Atma Vichara is "awareness watching awareness" but others who claim that one's attention should be fixed on the one who is watching. According to Humphrey's who was very close to Ramana was personally advised by Lord Ramana to fix one's attention on the one who is watching. Those were Humphrey's exact words*<.

There is absolutely no need to enquire into the Self, the Self is ever aware, but there is every need to enquire into the ego-self. The 'one who is watching' is indeed the upstart who needs attention. Bhagavan is very clear that in the enquiry, 'I' refers to the ego. As long as someone claims 'awareness' for themselves, there is a question begging.

"Mrs. D. said there were breaks in her awareness and desired to know how the awareness might be made continuous.

M.: Breaks are due to thoughts. You cannot be aware of breaks unless you think so. It is only a thought. Repeat the old practice, 'To whom do thoughts arise?' Keep up the practice until there are no breaks. Practice alone will bring continuity of awareness." (Talk 628)

Awareness watching awareness is 'I AM' awareness. This is a reflection of awareness in consciousness, also known as the witness consciousness. 'I AM' or 'I'-'I' (aham aham) sits at the threshold and is the expression of the pure mind, consisting of the primary thought, alone. When the mind looks outward, the kArakas* are used to explain the world. When the mind looks inwards it falters at the threshold, even I AM cannot cross, it falls away. The sphurana in the Heart is the expression of this 'I AM' awareness sitting on the threshold.

* kArakas – doers, the roles pertaining to action, creators of relation i.e. donor and recipient etc.

>*I want to thank you for the trouble you've gone to, to help me come to an understanding of the Vichara. I have read quite a few books on Ramana and his teachings and they have been of immense value in my search for the truth, however I need the guidance of an adept to advise me on whether I am doing the Vichara correctly. From what I've read of your letters, I get the impression you are someone who has firsthand experience of what you are saying. So I'll be grateful if you could tell whether I am doing the Vichara correctly. What I do is, try to fix my attention on that which is watching. When I am swept by a tide of thoughts I put the query "to whom are these thoughts" and so forth. I ignore the feeble thoughts and try to watch the watcher. Is this the correct method? Or should one cut off every thought with the query method? Which is the better method or can one use both methods depending on the prevailing mood. Incidentally in your letter you said one should attend to that which is watching as it is the ego-self and needs all the attention one can give it.*<

The very purpose of Self Enquiry is to focus the entire mind at its own source. Whenever one is distracted by thought (feeble or otherwise) we ask 'To whom does this thought appear?' The answer 'To me' is then resolved with the question 'Who am I?' This is not a question for the intellect. There is no answer. Any answer the intellect might give returns one to the question 'To whom does this thought appear?' The questioner himself is the answer. This is attention on the source. It is not, therefore, a case of one 'I' searching for another 'I'. Nor one 'I' watching another 'I'. The 'I' who searches is the 'I' searched for and both are the primal 'I'-thought. This 'I'-thought in turn dissolves, like the proverbial salt doll in the ocean, when it is held tight, through the process of Self Enquiry. In the Self there is no mind and no 'I'-thought, let alone any other thoughts.

Atma Vichara drives us home to the goal, where this primal 'I' is subsumed by the Atman, shining 'as It is', devoid of upAdhis [limiting adjuncts]. All suffering is reliant on the ignorance of the one fundamental fact that "in Reality, there are not two selves, there is only Self-abidance." "The thought 'I', 'mine' erroneously imposed on the body and senses, which are not the real Self, must be removed by the wise, by abiding as the real Self." (Vivekacudamani)

Misunderstanding this, all is misunderstood. Then self and other emanate relentlessly from our own consciousness. So, to reiterate, the questioning subverts the intellect and returns one, one-pointedly, to the Heart – i.e. Self-abidance. Here, the answer comes without words, like an irresistible pull, a quickening. This is an answer that, self-evidently, leaves no question begging (i.e. the question "To whom does this thought occur?" cannot be raised). This pull from the Heart is not under the control of the mind, all mind can do is keep itself emptied except for the thought "Who am I?" and where necessary "to whom do these thoughts arise?" in order that it remains open to the pull.

The Self needs no enquiry. All that is required is an emptying of the cloud-like thought processes which begin with the 'I'-thought. The senses can only perceive by the light they receive from the Self which abides in the Heart. The great tapas (austerity), which might at one time be seen as a penance sustained by great effort, is in reality the effortless return to the eternal fire of the Atman in the Heart.

The 'I'-thought brings all sorts in its train, selfhood, God, AUM, world, good, bad, birth, death, etc., every judgement that can be conceived of. Creation in all its glory. This simple process of Self Enquiry as described above, if applied with regular sustained, intensity, throughout the waking day, reverses the outward train of thought and concentrates attention on the creator of thought and the realisation that 'I' itself is the primal thought – ahamkara – without attributes. Standing at this threshold is self-abidance. It matters little that throughout the day the 'I' must become involved in thought processes as long as the mind is trained to return to the enquiry at the earliest moment available.

Remember any answer or experience that the mind can claim for its own such as 'I am watching', or 'I feel bliss' leaves the question begging. The purpose of enquiry is to suspend thought in order that 'I'-ness or Being alone is present. This is all one can do. At this point the 'I' will, in due course, sink into the Self. 'I am' is the beginning and the end of samsara. Even 'I am' is not the final answer.

7.2.2004 Anguish

>*My problem still is that when this is done for some time an incredible anguish arises and pushes me out again. Then Vichara is stopped – until the next pull comes to take up practice again. Atma Vichara can't be forgotten as it is the very essence of the teaching of Bhagavan, who is very near to my heart. Also – strange enough – it is felt that bhakti demands Vichara. Without Vichara no real bhakti here. So I*

try again and again – sometimes all the attempts seems to have no point at all.<

The feeling of anguish is not unusual when one practices enquiry. In fact it is inevitable. Self Enquiry draws out the latent tendencies in order that they can be summarily dealt with and this anguish is the ego's primary fear. Self-preservation is a powerful vasana which ego tends to misconstrue when faced with it in Vichara. It panics. Ideally when one comes across this it should be cut immediately with the question "To whom does this anguish appear?" This is the process of enquiry. This is easier said than done. The greatest stumbling block in enquiry is facing and overcoming this fear of death. Remember Bhagavan's experience. But if one can get through it....

However... Anguish is also a powerful and positive symptom of bhakti. The idea that 'I' might forget the presence of my Lord (or the quest for Self) for even a minute causes great anguish. But remember with forgetfulness of the Self comes the bliss of remembrance. If one can create an association of devotion with anguish then the fear is transformed into a longing. Whenever there is anguish one remembers and in that remembrance it is helpful to take to japa of your mantra for a while. Whenever there is anguish take to japa. Then, when ready, the feeling of great anguish provides the ideal vehicle for Atma Vichara to cut in. When Atma Vichara cuts in then true dedication begins. This is bhakti.

24.2.2004 Refraining from action

>I find a lot of people in this group saying that one should refrain from doing anything to free ourselves from the bondage of the self. One should be in a state of being and so on. I agree that all the misery in the world is a result of people trying to do this and that. However as long as the ego is there, man will continue to act. He cannot refrain from action. I think Ramana was very clear about this; he said we

need to make an effort. Papaji who has attained realisation says one should simply give up the notion of being in bondage. I think that is easier said than done. It is true that the maker of effort is the problem but he/she cannot be wished away. The Atma Vichara is an investigation into the 'I' or the maker of effort. I think if one goes about it in the prescribed way at some point one will get an insight into the nature of the ego and it will just drop away. When one stops identifying oneself with the limited self or the image we carry of ourselves then there is total freedom from fear or sorrow or whatever. Otherwise a visit to a good hypnotist is all we need to do to be rid of the 'I' notion. So let us not fool ourselves into believing realising the self can be so easy. One can of course sit quietly for a while without making any effort to do anything. It may work for a while but then the mind will get absorbed in 'doing'. Your boss rings you and tells you, you have a report to write up for the next day's meeting and your mind will start to run around in circles.<

This idea is primarily tAmasika and is, indeed, rife amongst the neo-advaitists. If it has been mentioned on this site it has also been countered elsewhere by the assertion that intense effort is needed by one who would 'break the bonds'. There are three categories of teacher, who correspondingly teach under the sway of the three gunas [tendencies of the mind] – sattva, rajas, and tamas [purity, passion and lethargy]. Where sAttvika principles are uppermost, the teaching of intense Self Enquiry predominates, along with bhakti leading to Self Enquiry. Where rAjasika tendencies are uppermost, the various yogas, hatha, raja, tantra, ritual worship etc. are taught. Where tAmasic tendencies are uppermost, lethargy leading to nihilism, holds sway. Unfortunately the simple injunction 'hrdi nama' – 'be still in the Heart' has been taken, by some, to mean that one should/can do nothing. This, then, changes what is clearly a sAttvika injunction into a tAmasika one. By means of sAttvika the other two are overcome. Of the three, the tAmasika tendencies are to be avoided. Remember the injunction 'Be still!' is an impetus to act.

Intense Vichara is essential. One must enquire into this individual as long as the sense of 'doing' is there. This leads to enquiry into the ego's aspect of seeking no less than the everyday aspects of judging, being still, etc. The task is one of growing attentiveness to the quest. This attentiveness is dependent on intensity of enquiry.

In the midst of work Vichara should become intense. Indeed work and the trials of working life are excellent fuel for Vichara.

30.3.2004

>*Ramana and others were often asked about this [the life as a householder] and gave the advice that the life of the householder should not be changed yet they themselves did not live this life.*<

It should be remembered that Sri Ramana left his home only after 'Realisation' not in order to attain realisation. He realised, albeit at a young age, in the midst of home and family. Of course, later an even larger family moved in and around him.

18.7.2004 AHAM- raduation

>*Taken from the following web page*
http://www.aham.com/enlightenment/index.html:
[note: This page has meanwhile been deleted.]

"*As far as we know, AHAM is the only organization or group anywhere in the world providing formal instruction in this powerful, but simple process brought to the world by Bhagavan Sri Ramana Maharshi, where, following your training, you receive personal formal guidance from a qualified Buddy who is an advanced graduate.*"

Are there any graduates here? I just heard that Sri V. Ganesan is recommending this. Can anyone confirm?<

Self Enquiry is indeed very simple. There is no need for unnecessary contrivance around the practice. It is freely available to one and all and has no copyright.

As you no doubt know, there is the very helpful Ramana Ashram in South India which abounds with information in the form of books, video tapes and, of course, 'The Mountain Path' magazine. This one institution is almost one too many. Why would one then build another institution? And in particular why a hierarchical institution involving graduation and advanced graduation? What would motivate such a thing? Who knows? It is reminiscent of the various 'life-management' type thingies which compete for 'punters' in a self-created marketplace. Surely this style of 'enquiry' can only bolster up the ego, as it waits and longs for the day it too can become a 'Buddy' and help those less well off than themselves.

Regarding Ganesan's 'recommendation', I am reminded of a very useful reply I received from him in the early 80s in response to a question about Bhagavan's possible reaction to western Indian-style spiritual organisations and their diverse views, in which he said, "... they only prove that the hunger of mankind for spiritual values can digest anything up to pebbles! You want to know what Bhagavan's views have been. He never started any such movement nor did he interfere in it."

8.12.2004

Vichara is the most intense activity of the entire mind to keep itself poised in pure Self-awareness.

5.7. 2005 Question about Self Enquiry

>I'm new to this group and a devotee of Sri Ramana. There

is one practical thing in His teachings that it is still not so clear to me. Sometimes he says that Atma Vichara is for the ones who are prepared – for the 'ripe souls' – and in other occasions he says that Atma Vichara is for anyone who fells drawn or attracted to such practice.

I personally feel very attracted to Self Enquiry – as I'm trying to practice it now – but for sure I'm not a 'ripe' or mature soul. So my question is: should I continue Atma Vichara or should I first devote myself to some "preliminary" practices and exercises (like meditation on my breath, neti-neti, "I am He", etc.)? Does anybody know any quotation of the Maharshi which clarifies this?<

Here are a few quotes which mention 'ripeness', as requested.

"Can this path of enquiry be followed by all aspirants? This is suitable only for ripe souls. The rest should follow different methods according to the state of their minds." (Spiritual Instruction)

"The Guru will go with the disciple in his own path and then gradually turn him onto the Supreme path at the ripe moment. Suppose a car is going at top speed. To stop it at once or to turn it at once would be attended with disastrous consequences." (Mudaliar: Day by Day, 22.11.1945 Afternoon)

"D. Cannot Grace hasten ripeness in the seeker?

M. Leave it all to the Master. Surrender to Him without reserve. One of two things must be done; either surrender yourself, because you realize your inability and need a Higher Power to help you; or investigate into the cause of misery, go into the Source and so merge in the Self. Either way, you will be free from misery. God or Guru never forsakes the devotee who has surrendered himself." (Maharshi's Gospel, p. 36)

"D: Although I have listened to the explanation of the characteristics of enquiry in such great detail, my mind has not gained even a little peace. What is the reason for this?

M: The reason is the absence of strength or one-pointedness of the mind.

D: What is the reason for the absence of mental strength?

M: The means that make one qualified for enquiry are meditation, yoga, etc. One should gain proficiency in these through graded practice, and thus secure a stream of mental modes that is natural and helpful. When the mind that has in this manner become ripe, listens to the present enquiry, it will at once realize its true nature which is the Self, and remain in perfect peace, without deviating from that state. To a mind which has not become ripe, immediate realization and peace are hard to gain through listening to enquiry. Yet, if one practices the means for mind-control for some time, peace of mind can be obtained eventually." (Self Enquiry, Q&A 19 and 20)

23.8.2007 Why does it matter?

>*On the path of Atma Vichara (or any other path) there is a change or movement from dvaita to advaita, from ajnana to jnana, from darkness to enlightenment etc... This change need to happen somewhere. Now my understanding that everything that does change, is not real, because if it changes it must have a start and therefore an end and therefore it is not eternal i.e. NOT REAL. Now, my question is, if the whole path is not real why does it matter, if I do an effort to follow a certain sadhana or not, if at the bottom line it doesn't have any meaning because it is still in the realm of maya. Some were deep just next to 'I', I have a feeling that it does matter if you do it or not, but I cannot understand why. I would appreciate some insight into the matter.<*

It doesn't!

Atma Vichara is dvaita (dual). It is a movement in ajnana (ignorance). Neither advaita (non-dual) nor jnana (knowledge) move. Ego might be tempted by sadhana, Self has no need for it. This is the paradox.

The idea about movement from darkness to light is simply mind's play. When the obstruction vanishes, it takes the shadows with it. Light's brightness was ever unaffected.

For Vichara, no sadhana (spiritual discipline) is required other than the discipline of remembrance. Since this discipline is innate, in truth, there is no discipline, as such.

"Reality is simply the loss of the ego. Destroy the ego by seeking its identity. Because the ego is no entity it will automatically vanish and Reality will shine forth by itself. This is the direct method. Whereas all other methods are done, only retaining the ego. In those paths there arise so many doubts and the eternal question remains to be tackled finally. But in this method the final question is the only one and it is raised from the very beginning. No sadhanas are necessary for engaging in this quest." (from Talk 146)

"Sadhana is only to get rid of the bodily and other illusions which are in the way of the self standing up as Self. This delusion arises only by thinking that this bodily world is real, instead of looking at the Self, which is real. Sadhana is only to get rid of this illusion. Otherwise, why should there be sadhana for the Self to attain its own Self? He who has realised his own Self does not recognize anything else." (Nagamma: Letters, 23.8.1946)

18.9.2007

>*There has always been a lot of misunderstanding when it comes to… How is the Vichara to be done. I try to be attentive to my awareness or my sense of self or being or aliveness. Is that the right way.*<

It may be that the confusion is caused because 'I' am never clever enough to theorise on Vichara (Self Enquiry). It is certainly the case that when I write on such things I get tied in knots. I lay the whole thing out for all to see, step back to admire it, but inevitably the very I, that is the subject of the enquiry, stands watching, unnoticed.

The 'I' that tries is the 'I' that is the subject of enquiry. Whatever this 'I' tries to do is mindstuff.

Our assumed awareness is a mere reflection of true unassumed awareness. When one walks over the brink of a hill to be met, unexpectedly, by an unbelievable, breath-taking display of natural beauty, that is pure awareness. In that immediate moment there is no interfering ego.... The same can be said of other sudden and unexpected situations – horror, fear, surprise etc. etc. – which one comes upon denuded of ego, if only for a moment.

Then the ego pops up to describe, remember and catalogue, and the moment is lost. No matter how often the moment's memory is rehearsed, it is only reflected memory.

The Enquiry (Vichara) is an enquiry into ego. It is not an enquiry into Self. It is not an enquiry into awareness. It as an enquiry into the thief which has stolen awareness. It is an enquiry into the insentient tool which, although unable to work without unseen backing, has come to believe that it is the Self.

20.9.2007

>*Thanks for your response. I don't know if you've read the Path of Ramana by Sadhu Om. He says the way to do Vichara is by being grounded in the 'I feeling'. There is an awareness in us of which we are all aware besides our thoughts and feelings. We know we are conscious. So I watch my consciousness. This I have been told by some Ramana devotees is the correct way. So there is much confu-*

sion on this subject and a lack of proper understanding as to what constitutes Vichara. The first book I read of Ramana about 10 years ago was by Arthur Osbourne. I think he recommended the verbal questioning method. If it is an inquiry it has to be done verbally or one just has to watch one's consciousness intently. So your comments are invited and I hope I get a few more opinions on the subject as I think this needs to be cleared to everyone's satisfaction.<

The 'I' feeling/sense is quite simply the root of ego.

From Mudaliar: Day by Day, 31.5.1946: "... so long as there is the feeling 'I', it must have a source from whence it came."

If one remains attached to this root thoughts are kept at bay. The primary means of remaining here is by enquiring as and when mind drifts and allows spurious thoughts to arise. This is the point of the "Who am I?" method of Enquiry. If mind drifts into the mindstuff of thought it gets nudged back by the Enquiry. If mind sits still there is no need for the Enquiry question, one simply waits. Ego can go no further under its own steam.

From Lakshmana Sarma's 'Maha Yoga': "When the sense of 'I am the body' arises, then the notions of 'you' and 'he' also arise; but when, by the Quest of the Truth underlying the 'I', the 'I'-sense is put an end to, then the notions of 'you' and 'he' also cease; that which then shines as the Sole Remainder is the true Self." (p. 69)

The 'I'-sense goes out as a thief. The whole point of Enquiry is to stop this thief from venturing out willy-nilly and stealing 'experiences'.

Again from 'Maha Yoga': "...ego has an element of reality mixed up in it, namely the light of Consciousness, manifest as 'I am'. This 'I am', we know, is real, because it is the part that is constant and unchanging. We need to reject the unreal part, the sheaths or bodies, and take the remainder, the pure 'I am'. This 'I am' is a clue to the finding of the real Self. By holding on to this clue, the Sage tells us, we can surely find the Self. He once compared the seeker of the Self to a dog seeking his master, from whom he had been parted. The dog has something to guide him, namely the master's scent. By following the scent, leaving everything else, he ultimately finds his master. The 'I am' in the ego-sense is just like the master's scent for the dog. It is the only clue the seeker has for finding the Self. But it is an infallible clue. He must get and keep hold of it, fix his mind on it to the exclusion of all other things. It will then surely take his mind to the Self, the source of the 'I am'." (p. 142)

On page 146, Sri K. Lakshmana Sarma continues: "The Quest of the real Self consists in gathering together all the energies of body and mind by banishing all alien thoughts, and then directing all those energies into a single current, namely the resolve to find the answer to the question 'Who am I?' The question may also take the form of 'Whence am I?' 'Who am I?' means 'What is the Truth of me?'; 'Whence am I?' means 'What is the Source of the sense of self in the ego?'"

Lakshmana Sarma received one on one tutelage for years from Maharshi. Surely, this record must count for something.

21.9.2007

It is the antithesis of the "everything is just hunky dory let's stick it all in the pot and see what comes out" brigade. The one who wants to have all the options, melting them down into egoistic smoothie gunk, is the very one to be enquired into.

Many of the methods that have been discussed may be valuable aids to Vichara... however, when all the various aids are taken to be the practice, the practice, itself, is ignored. The aids must be understood for what they are. As long as these methods do not engage with the ego, they are not Vichara.

Vichara practice engages with the ego-I. It does not go off looking for awareness, or contemplating breath, it engages with the one who has decided that such a search is the true practice. Who looks? Who is aware? Vichara engages with and removes this ultimately fictitious thief, the one that searches, the one that is aware. He will no longer be there in the final cut.

28.11.2007 The Path of Sri Ramana by Sri Sadhu Om

>*If Self Enquiry is a thought-process done by the mind [where mind = 'I am so and so', the ego-sense OR the false first person (poyyaana thanmai uNarvu) awareness], then this process of SE will be possible only when performed in isolation (when the attention is not on the worldly activities).*

However, Sri Bhagavan (and consequently, devotees like Sri Sadhu Om et. al.) have mentioned on more than one occasion that a) Self Enquiry can be done anywhere at any time even while engaged in other (worldly) activities & b) the 'path' and the 'goal' are 'one and the same'. Multiple verses in Ulladu Narpadu delineate the process, however, as you can see, there is still confusion here...<

Self Enquiry can only be done by mind. No other entity requires it. If this fundamental fact is not grasped, all is missed. Self Enquiry must become all-consuming and can be done at all times.

The simple fact is that only mind requires Vichara, only mind can perform Vichara. If a writer claims otherwise he is a fool.

As Chadwick said "This process has often been misunderstood, though actually Bhagavan's teaching is quite clear. In this search one is not to seek for some transcendental 'I-Absolute', but for the ego itself and the point where it arises. Find this, the ego automatically drops away and one then knows there is nothing but the Self. It is like following a stream to its source through the hills, and when one has reached that point whence it arises the stream itself will no longer exist. Source, mind, ego are one and the same and cannot exist apart from each other. The mind cannot know the Self, for how can it know that which is beyond mind?" (Sadhu Arunachala, p. 62-63)

The ideas of enlightenment and need for Vichara belong to ego alone. When ego searches within the foothills of its own existence and finds its source it settles down exhausted, vanquished. At that point there is no longer any need for Vichara. Only wayward mind needs the map of Vichara. Self is ever self-aware of its whereabouts.

29.12.2007 The 'I'-feeling

>*I think I have an idea what the 'I'-feeling that Ramana talked about is but I would like to know from other members what they think the 'I'-feeling is. I think practicing Ramana's method of Vichara is just staying with the 'I'-feeling. The reason I've posted to the group is to verify whether others think the same thing. If they have their own interpretation I should like to hear what it is.*<

There are various references to 'I'-ness/'I'-feeling/'I'-sense, for example,

"Is not the sense of 'I' natural to all beings, expressed in all their feelings as 'I came', 'I went', 'I did', or 'I was'? On questioning what this is, we find that the body is identified with 'I' because movements and similar functions pertain to the body. Can the body then be this 'I'-consciousness? It was not there before birth, it is composed of the five elements, it is absent in sleep, and it (eventually) becomes a corpse. No, it cannot be. This sense of 'I', which arises in the body for the time being, is otherwise called the ego, ignorance, illusion, impurity, or individual self. The purpose of all the scriptures is this enquiry (into the Self). It is declared in them that the annihilation of the ego-sense is Liberation." (from Self Enquiry Essay available in "Words of Grace, p. 3)

"It is the ineradicable ego, the 'I-ness' in each of us, which is responsible for the perpetuation of this maya with all its attendant sufferings and disenchantments. ... So all that you have to do is to get to this I, the real I behind your seeming I, for then you are rid forever of the illusive 'I'-ness and all is attained, since you stay thenceforward at one with That which is you; that's all." (Surpassing Love and Grace, p. 218)

From Talk 54: "If the present 'I'-ness vanishes, the discovery is complete. What remains over is the pure Self."

From [Nagamma] Letter 83: "Bhagavan has written in his Unnadhi Nalupadhi, verse 14: 'If it is said that there is the first person 'I' then there are the second and third persons 'you' and 'he'. When the real nature of the first person is known and the 'I' feeling disappears, the 'you' and the 'he' disappear simultaneously, and that which shines as the only One becomes the natural state of the ultimate reality."

29.12.2007 The 'I'-feeling

>*Although at the relative level we may name this a 'feeling' (the 'I'-feeling) there is a risk of pursuing a 'state' of mind (that will always be within ignorance and duality anyway) rather than the dissolution of the relative mind, or ego-sense, and the 'experience' of non-dual consciousness WITHOUT any 'experiencer'. According to this view I*

would always prefer to speak about the 'I'-thought than the 'I'-feeling, since the 'I'-thought is the 'root' of the 'I'-feeling (from my understanding point of view).<

Indeed. It is commonplace to erroneously pursue a state of mind, in the name of Vichara. There seems to be a fundamental misconception that ego-I can watch 'I am I' ('I-I') and that this is Vichara. Not only is this not Vichara, it is also impossible. The Quest demands only that the source of ego (i.e. the 'I'-thought) be held in readiness for eviction. Ego goes no further.

With regard to this ego removal there is an interesting passage in Sri Sarma's 'Maha Yoga': "The Self is the pure 'I AM', the only thing that is self-manifest; by Its light all the world is lighted up. But It seems to be unknown, and to need to be known, because It is obscured by the world and the ego. What is needed is to remove these. The Sage explains this by the analogy of a room that is encumbered with unwanted lumber. If space be wanted, all that is needful is to clear out the lumber; no space has to be brought in from outside. So too, the ego-mind and its creations have to be emptied out, and then the Self alone would remain, shining without hindrance. What is loosely called 'knowing the Self' is really being egoless, and the Self. Thus the Sage does not know the Self; he is the Self."

BIBLIOGRAPHY

Abhishiktananda: Secrets of Arunachala, 1997

The Collected Works of Sri Ramana Maharshi. – 9th ed. – Tiruvannamalai, 2004

Conscious Immortality: Conversations with Sri Ramana Maharshi. – 2nd ed. – Tiruvannamalai, 1998

Godman, David: Be As You Are. – London, 1986

Hewitt, James: Teach yourself Yoga. – Ntc Pub Group; English Language edition (January 1995)

Mudaliar, Devaraja: Day by Day with Bhagavan. – Tiruvannamalai, 2011

Maharshi's Gospel. – 10th ed. – Tiruvannamalai, 1987

Muruganar: Ramana Mandiram, Tiruvannamalai, 1968

Nagamma, Suri: Letters from Sri Ramanasramam. – Tiruvannamalai, 2011

Nisargadatta: I Am That. – 16th printing. – Durham, 2009

Ramana Maharshi: The Collected Works of Sri Ramana Maharshi. – 9th ed. – Tiruvannamalai, 2004

Ramana Maharshi: Who am I? – 24th ed. – Tiruvannamalai, 2008

Ramana Maharshi: Words of Grace (including "Who am I", Self-Enquiry, Spiritual Instruction). – 3rd ed. – Tiruvannamalai 1996

Sadhu Arunachala (Major Chadwick): A Sadhu's Reminiscences of Ramana Maharshi. – 5th ed. – Tiruvannamalai, 1994

Sarma, L. Lakshmana : Maha Yoga. – Tiruvannamalai, 2002

Sarma, L. Lakshmana: Ramanaparavidyopanishad. – Tiruvannamalai, 2006

Sastri, Gaurinath: The Philosophy of Word and Meaning, Calcutta: Sanskrit College, 1959

Sri Ramana Gita. – Tiruvannamalai, 2003

Subbaramayya, G.V.: Sri Ramana Reminiscences. – Tiruvannamalai, 1994

Surpassing Love and Grace. – Tiruvannamalai, 2001

Tripura Rahasya. – Tiruvannamalai, 2006

V. Ganeshan: Moments Remembered. – Tiruvannamalai, 1994

Venkataramiah, Munagala: Talks with Sri Ramana Maharshi. – 13th ed. – Tiruvannamalai, 2013